AFTER WORLD'S END

By
JACK WILLIAMSON

I0616908

ARMCHAIR FICTION
PO Box 4369, Medford, Oregon 97504

For more information about Armchair Books and products, visit our
website at…

www.armchairfiction.com

Or email us at…

armchairfiction@yahoo.com

IT WAS THE ERA OF THE ROBOT CORPORATION

When scientist and explorer, Dr. Barry Horn, was recruited to be the world's first rocketeer, he was reticent…until he received a vision from his late wife imploring him to go.

He set off for Venus, but something went horribly wrong, and he wound up in a state of suspended animation…unable to move, but subjected to visions of the marches of time. He witnessed his descendants going into space, creating the first living robot, and watched the rise of the Robot Corporation and its ongoing and systematic destruction of mankind.

When Barry finally awakened he found himself with a great and terrible burden. He—with the aid of the Dondara Stone—was saddled with the task of destroying Malgarth and his robot minions. But first he had to find and rescue the Custodian of the Stone…if she was still alive.

FOR A COMPLETE SECOND NOVEL, TURN TO PAGE 131

CAST OF CHARACTERS

BARRY HORN
He took off as a young adventurer, but when he awakened he was an old man who was faced with saving all life in the universe.

KEL "THE FALCON" ARAN
This Robin Hood of space was determined to save his lady love and put an end to the evil reign of the Robot Corporation.

VEREL ERIN
She was chosen to be the Custodian of the Dondara Stone. She vowed to keep the stone safe, but would it keep her alive?

MALGARTH
This metallic monstrosity was created with a living brain, but the scientist forgot a heart…

GUGON KUL
He was an Admiral of the Galactic Guard who tenaciously pursued the Falcon…but was always just one step behind.

TEDRON DU
He was the Emperor of the Galaxy, but he sold out his people for the security that the Robot Corporation gave.

SETSI
This strange little creature was a psychic silicic life-form, who had a penchant for rum.

CHAPTER ONE
The Rocket Astronaut

"Mought dis beof int'rest to yuh, suh?"

The advertisement was pointed out to be by a friendly elevator operator at the Explorer's Club. Placed in the classified columns of the *New York Standard*, for October 8, 1938, it ran:

WANTED: Vigorous man, with training and experience in scientific exploration, to undertake dangerous and unusual assignment. Apply in person, this evening, 6 to 10.
Dr. Hilaire Crosno, Hotel Crichton.

That sounded good. I had been in New York just twice too long. Always, when I had come back from the long solitudes of desert or jungle, the first fortnight on Broadway was a promised paradise, and the second began to be hell.

I gave the grinning boy a dollar, stuffed an envelope with credentials, downed another stiff peg of whiskey, and walked into the glittering chromium lobby on the stroke of six. My inquiry for Dr. Crosno worked magic on the supercilious clerk.

Crosno proved to be a big man, with huge bald head and deep, sunken, dark, magnetic eyes. The tension of his mouth hinted of some hidden strain, and extreme pallor suggested that, physically, he was near the breaking point.

"Barry Horn?" His voice was deep and calm—yet somehow terrible with a haunting echo of panic. He was shuffling through my references. "Qualifications seem sound enough. Your doctorate?"

"Honorary," I told him. "For a pyramid I dug out of the jungle in Quintana Roo." I glanced at the room's austere luxury, still trying to size him up. "Just what, Doctor, is your 'unusual assignment'—?"

Majestically, he ignored my question. Gray eyes studied me.

"You look physically fit, but there must be an examination," he checked a card in his hand. "You know something of astronomy and navigation?"

"Once I sailed the hull of a smashed seaplane a thousand miles across the Indian Ocean."

The big head nodded, slowly.

"You could leave at once, for an—indefinite time?"

I said *yes.*

"Dependents?"

"I've a son, four years old." The bitterness must have shadowed my voice. "But he's not dependent on me. His mother is dead, and her people convinced the courts that a footloose explorer wasn't the proper guardian for little Barry."

Dona Carridan was again before me, tall and proud and lovely. The one year I had known her, when she had tempestuously left her wealthy family to go with me to Mesopotamia, had been the happiest of my life. Suddenly I was trembling again with the terror of the plane crash in the desert; our son born in an Arab's tent; Dona, far from medical aid, dying in agony...

"Then, Horn," Crosno was asking, "you're ready to cut loose from—everything?"

"I am."

He stared at me. His long-fingered hands, so very white, were trembling with the papers. Suddenly he said, decisively:

"All right, Horn. You'll do."

"Now," I demanded again, "what's the job?"

"Come," he rose. "I'll show you."

A huge, shabby old car carried us uptown, across the George Washington bridge, and up the river to a big, wooded estate. A uniformed butler let us into an immense old house, as shabby as the car.

"My library."

Guiding me back through the house, Crosno paused as if he wished me to look into the room. An intricate planetarium was suspended from the ceiling. Glass cases held models of things that I took to be experimental rockets. The big man silently pointed out shelves of books on explosives, gases, aerodynamic design, celestial mechanics, and astro-physics. Startled, I met Crosno's piercing eyes.

"Yes, Horn," he told me. "You're to be the first rocketeer in history."

"Eh?" I stared at him. "You don't mean—outer space?"

I wondered at the shadow of bleak despair that had fallen across his cragged, dead-white features.

"Come," he said. "Into the garden."

The night had a frosty brilliance. Moonlight spilled over the trees and neglected lawns; and Venus, westward, hung like a solitary drop of molten silver. I stopped with a gasp of wonderment.

Weathered boards were stacked around the foundation of a dismantled building. Upon the massive concrete floor, shimmering under the moon, stood a tall bright cylinder. Bell-flared muzzles cast black shadows below. A frail ladder led up its shimmering side, sixty feet at least, to the tiny black circle of an entrance port.

"That—" A queer, stunned feeling had seized me. "That—"

"That is my rocket." The deep voice was ragged, choked. "The *Astronaut.*" His face was bleak with agony. "I've given twenty years of my life to go, Horn. And now I must send another. An unsuspected weakness of my heart—couldn't survive the acceleration."

The white lofty cylinder was suddenly a dreadful thing. There is a feeling that comes upon me, definite as a grasping hand and a whispered warning. Sometimes I have not heeded it, and always in the end, found myself face to face with death. Now that feeling said, *There lies ghastly peril.*

Slowly I turned to the tall pale man.

"I'm an explorer, all right, Crosno," I said. "I've taken risks, and I'm willing to take more. But if you think I'm going to climb into that contraption, and be blown off to the moon—"

The hurt on his gaunt bloodless face stopped my voice.

"Not the moon, Horn." A gesture of his long arm carried my gaze from the mottled lunar disk, westward to the evening star. "To Venus," he said. "First."

I caught my breath, staring in awe at the white planet.

"The range of the *Astronaut*," he said, "should enable you to reach there, land, spend several months in exploration, and time your return to reach Earth safely at the next conjunction—if you are very lucky."

His dark, magnetic eyes probed me.

"What do you say, Horn?"

"Give me a little while," I said. "Alone."

I walked out of the garden, and up through dark-massed trees to the open summit of a little hill beyond. The autumn constellations flamed near and bright above; yet I could hear crickets below, and a distant frog; could sometimes catch a haunting flower-odor from the meadows.

A long time I stood there, gazing up at Venus and the stars. Earth, I thought, had not been kind to me; life, since Dona's death, had seemed all weariness and pain. Yet— could I leave it, willingly and forever?

Indecision tortured me, until I saw a shooting star. A white stellar bullet, out of the black mystery of space, it flamed down across Cassiopeia and Perseus; and somehow its fire rekindled in me that vague and yet intense knowledge-lust that is the heart of any scientist.

But I couldn't understand the thing that happened then. It was a waking dream, queerly real, that banished the sky and the hill. Standing in sudden darkness, I saw a woman who lay sleeping in a long crystal box. Her slim, long-limbed form was beautiful, and it seemed hauntingly familiar.

She seemed to wake, as I watched. She looked at me, with wide eyes that were violet-black, and filled with an urgent dread. She half rose, in her thick mantle of dark, red-gleaming hair. And her voice spoke to me from the crystal casket, saying:

"Go, Barry Horn! You must go."

In another instant, the vision was ended. The soft night sounds and the moonlight were about me again, and the autumnal breeze swept a cool fragrance from the meadows. I caught a deep breath, and wrestled with enigma.

The woman in the crystal had been, unmistakably, Dona Carridan!

Scientific training has left me little superstition. Walking back down the hill, I wondered if I had been trying too hard to drown in alcohol my bitter loneliness for her. It must have been hallucination.

But her beauty and her terror had been too real to ignore. I knew that I must go.

I went back to Crosno, waiting beside the rocket, and told him my decision. But something caught my throat as I asked him, "When?"

Venus was overhauling Earth in its orbit, he said, approaching inferior conjunction. His calculations were based on a start at three the next Sunday morning.

"Four days," he said. "Can you be ready?"

I said I could. And there was oddly little to do. I packed and stored a few possessions, called on my attorney, and then went back to study the controls and mechanism of the rocket.

The greatest danger, Crosno said, would be from the Cosmic Rays. They would penetrate the rocket. He made me take a drug to guard against them.

"It was compounded for me by a great radiologist," he told me. "A modification of the Petrie formula. The base of it is a new uranium salt that seems less poisonous than most. We're trying to neutralize the effects of one type of radiation with those of another."

The stuff was a greenish liquid. He injected it into my arm, twice daily. The only apparent effect was a feverish restlessness. I was unable to sleep, despite a mounting, crushing fatigue.

On the last night, when all was tested and ready, Crosno sent me up to my room. But the torture of that insomnia drove me to slip out of the house. I walked for many hours across the slumbering countryside. The world slept beneath a gibbous moon. Far off, a train rumbled and whistled. A dog barked in the distance. The air was spiced with autumn. A slow dull regret rose in me that I must leave all this—all the Earth.

I thought of Dona, dead. Suddenly my bitterness toward her people seemed a childish, petulant thing. I wanted to make peace with them. For Dona's sake, and little Barry's. I wanted to find a telephone, and call them, and talk to little Barry.

But it was long past midnight—too late to wake the child. I recalled that strange dream, hallucination, whatever it was, of Dona in the crystal box. And a sudden breathless eagerness turned me back to Crosno's place. He was waiting about the rocket, alarmed by my absence.

"I couldn't sleep," I told him. "That damned drug—"

"I was afraid—" he said anxiously, "—you've just ten minutes."

I climbed the spidery ladder, pulled myself through the small round man-hole into the cramped tiny control room, and screwed the airtight plate into position behind me. Outside, Crosno dived into a sand-bagged shelter.

Trying to forget that I was sitting on enough high explosive to blow me to kingdom come, I kept my eyes on an illuminated chronometer. My hands were cold and trembling on the three levers connected to the three rocket motors. At last the needle touched the hour, and I pulled the firing levers.

The sound was the shriek of a million typhoons. The rocket drove upward like a giant sledge. I could see the hurricane of fire spread blue against the dark ground. It covered Crosno's shelter.

Then all the Earth was whisked downward. Enduring that hell of deafening sound and battering force, I held the three levers down for seeming eternities. At last the velometer showed eight miles a second—enough to escape the gravity of Earth—and I shut off the motors.

A strange peace filled the tiny room. The silence and the apparent want of motion—for I had no sense of the rocket's terrific velocity—cradled me in delicious comfort. I set out to discover my position and course.

The moonlight Earth became visibly a huge round ball, floating amid the stars, slowly receding. The moon was a queer globe of harsh light and blackness, drifting beside my path. The Sun came finally into view from behind the Earth, so intolerably bright that I slid the metal screens over the ports toward it.

A long time I searched for Venus, which also had been hidden when I started. Bright, tiny point, I could hardly realize that it was another world, rushing toward our rendezvous with a speed greater than my own.

I was gumbling for sextant and slide rule and tables, to try to discover and correct the direction of my flight, when I first perceived the prickling of my flesh. A queerly painful feeling, burning through every tissue.

It must be the Cosmic Rays, I knew; those intense, space-pervading radiations from which the Earth is shielded only by miles of atmosphere. Perhaps I hadn't taken enough of Crosno's drug. With numbed hands I found the little hypodermic clipped to the wall, shot another heavy dose into my arm.

"No sleep now," I muttered wearily. "Not for a million miles!"

And I reached again for the sextant. For the white point of Venus was incredibly tiny, and thirty million miles away. The slightest deviation, I knew, would carry me thousands of miles wide of the target—perhaps to fall into the merciless furnace of the Sun.

But a queer, deadly numbness had followed the prickling. I felt a terrible sudden pressure of sleep. All the accumulated fatigue of those sleepless nights and days poured over me resistlessly.

I knew it wouldn't do to sleep—not until the course of the *Astronaut* had been calculated and corrected. A delay of minutes, even, might be fatal. With dead hands I struggled to adjust the sextant, fighting for life itself.

But the instrument slipped from my fingers. *The drug,* I thought. *Some reaction with the Cosmic Rays; an effect that Crosno had not anticipated. Missing…Venus…*

I slept.

CHAPTER TWO
The Conquest of the Stars

Uranium is a strange element, slightly understood. The heaviest natural element, it is the mother of a dozen others, even of magic radium. For its radioactive atom breaks down to form a chain of other elements—slowly in nature, with great speed as a nuclear bomb.

The uranium salts in that drug must have been responsible for my sleep.

At first there was only blank darkness.

Then out of it spoke a low, clear voice, terribly familiar—
—the voice of Dona Carridan and of the woman in the crystal box—calling urgently:

"Barry! Wake up, Barry Horn."

Then, out of trembling awe, I came back to a queer sort of subliminal awareness. Something I had never experienced before, it was the sort of perception that might be possessed by a truly disembodied mind—yet I had an odd feeling that it came to me through the voice that had called.

I remember reading of Rhine's famous experiments in "parapsychology." It must have been some phenomenon of what he calls extra-sensory perception, independent of nerves and sense organs, even of distance and time, that came to my sleeping brain.

It was a thing of thought alone. I was aware of my stiff body, slumped awkwardly over the controls of the silent, hurtling rocket. But the rigid flesh seemed no more real, no more a part of me, than the run-down chronometer or the cold rocket muzzles.

It was nothing of feeling or hearing or sight, and I knew that it was guided by another mind. Gradually it spread, an expanding sphere of awareness. It went beyond the rocket. I perceived Venus, and knew that indeed I had missed it.

The *Astronaut* was plunging toward the Sun!

Filled with an oddly vague alarm, I made a dim effort to move my body, long enough at least to correct the course of the rocket. But that proved altogether hopeless. And I soon forgot all danger, in the wonder of this new perception.

For I *had* missed Venus!

Crosno, I knew, had allowed eighty-nine days for me to reach intersection with its orbit. But already the cloud-shrouded globe of it had flashed back beside me, fleet as a silver shadow.

Three months gone!

The next instant, I thought, the rocket would strike the Sun! No, its original momentum carried it by. Yet the star of day filled an enormous fiery circle. The rocket flung about it like a stone on a string. Then, like the stone when the string breaks, it hurtled outward again into space.

The incredible truth came slowly to me—

The *Astronaut* was now a comet!

Some freak of celestial mechanics, while my numb hands slept on the firing levers, had flung it into an elliptic orbit. A sealed vault flying into the void, like the fabulous coffin of Mohammed, it was destined to flash again around the Sun, recede, drop again...forever!

All that cycle happened, with the thought.

Years, I knew, had passed. Time was rushing by me like a river. I could sense the swift rotation of the planets, their deliberate orbital swing, even the northward drift of the whole solar system. And yet again I was amazed by the range and vividness of this new intuition.

For, thinking of Crosno back upon the Earth, I suddenly could see his place beside the Hudson, as clearly as if I had been floating above the trees. The old house was shabbier than ever, sagging. Behind it stood a tall white monument, upon which I read: *Hilaire Crosno, 1889=1961.*

Sixty-one!

Already it was twenty years and more since I had left the Earth. And it seemed the merest instant! For a moment I was stunned. Then I wanted desperately to know what the decades had done to my son. And that uncanny perception showed him to me.

He was an old man, already, walking slowly in a garden. Lingering beside his halting steps were a youth and a bright-haired girl—his children, I knew. The girl caught her brother's arm, and begged him anxiously:

"Barry, you—you mustn't! The danger's too ghastly. You'll only be lost in space—like grandfather!"

"But, Sis!" protested this slim new Barry Horn. "You don't understand." He looked up to the old man.

My son smiled, and patted his daughter's golden head. "Let him go, Dona," he said softly. "Danger was always food and drink to the Horns—we would die without it. Anyhow, Barry has a better rocket than my father's."

With that unaccountable perception, I watched my grandson enter his craft, smaller and trimmer than the *Astronaut;* I saw him fly safely out to the moon and back. And I felt a swift glow of pride to see men, and men bearing the name of Horn, moving toward conquest of the stars.

Driven now by haste and pain, I cannot set down all my scattered observations through the generations and the centuries that followed. But I watched the history of man and the lives of my children.

I saw other, greater ships put out into space—powered, presently, with the new space-contractor drive invented by Benden Horn. I saw colonies set up on the deserts of Mars, on the great polar islands of Venus. I saw the first interstellar ship bear its load of human colonists toward the newly discovered planets of Sirius—and I was proud that her captain bore the name of Horn.

Men multiplied and grew mighty. Commerce followed exploration, and commerce brought interstellar law. For a hundred thousand years—that seemed, in that uncanny sleep, no more than an hour—I watched the many-sided struggle between a score of interplanetary federations and the armada of space pirates that once menaced them all.

Still the *Astronaut* pursued its lonely course about the Sun. An insignificant fleck of tarnished metal, among all the millions of meteoric fragments, it was marked in the space charts as a menace to astrogation, given a wide berth by all shipping. And still my body slept.

Spreading from star to star, the rival federations drove the pirates at last to the fringes of the galaxy, and then turned back upon one another in ruthless galactic war. For ten thousand years ten million planets were drenched with blood. Democracies and communes crumbled before dictatorship. And one dictator, at last, was triumphant. The victorious League of Ledros became the Galactic Empire.

A universal peace and new prosperity came to the world of stars. Enlightened Emperors restored democratic institutions, Ledros, the capital planet, became the heart of interstellar civilization. Science resumed a march long interrupted. And among the scientists of the new renaissance, I saw a man who bore the name Bari Horn.

It was on the exhausted, war-scarred Earth that I found this namesake. His laboratory was a transparent dome that crowned a ray-blackened hill. Amid huge, enigmatic mechanisms, his body was straight and slim, and I fancied in his features some likeness to my own.

Bari Horn stood watching a huge crystal beaker set in a nest of gleaming equipment. It held, bathed in a purple, luminescent solution, a dark, deeply convoluted mass— something that looked like a monster brain! A golden ray shone upon it. Drop by drop, from a thin glass tube, the man was adding a blood-red liquid. And suddenly the needle of a meter, beside the beaker, which had been motionless, began to tremble with a slow, irregular pulsation.

My namesake turned suddenly pale, and caught his breath. "Dondara!" he shouted in elation. "Dondara—it responds!" He ran out of the dome, and came back pulling a girl by the hand. And I knew, through the wonder of that perception, that she was Dondara Keradin, the gifted research assistant of this man, and his dearly beloved.

But a blade of agony cleft my heart. For her slim beauty was terribly familiar. Her dark hair had that glint of red I knew so well, and her eyes were the true violet I had seen only in my dead wife, and in that crystal vision. She *was* Dona Carridan, and the woman in the crystal!

A bright flame of hope burned at my old skepticism of reincarnation. Was Dona born again? Had I slept these thousand centuries to find her? A weary despair quenched that hope. For if she had been reborn, so had I, in this eager experimenter beside her.

"Come, Dondara, darling!" Bari Horn was gasping. "All the others were mere machines. But this responds—*intelligently!* Watch the needle. It spells a message—a request for different food-chemicals!"

The lovely girl looked unwillingly at the black, faintly quivering mass in the crystal vessel. A slow horror widened and glazed her eyes.

"I don't like it, Bari," she whispered. "It's—*bestial!*"

"The others were," said the flushed experimenter. "But this is an actual brain. Its cells and fibers are of metal colloids, sheathed in synthetic myelin. A robot brain—finer and quicker than a man's!"

Her face was white. "I don't like it," she insisted. "Why make a mechanical brain better than a man's, Bari—when the brains of men have already done so much?"

"Because there is so much yet to be done," Bari Horn told her. "Men have no more than explored the Galaxy—Nature is not yet and perhaps never will be fully conquered. My robot technomatons will be a powerful ally.

"A man's brain is stupid. It learns slowly and with effort. It fumbles. It is clogged or diverted with emotion. It forgets. And finally, when it has acquired a little learning and a little skill, it dies altogether.

"But this brain—I'm going to name it Malgarth, from the first letters the needle spelled out—is quick. No emotion will disturb its delicate processes. It will never tire, never forget—never die! Barring accident, it can survive a million years, always growing, gaining knowledge, solving problems that would baffle a whole race of men. It will be itself a library and museum of all knowledge, stored up to aid mankind.

"There are fine machines, already. Now my robot brains can tend them, and men will be set free."

"Free?" The girl stared at him, a horror in her eyes. "Or enslaved—to your robots?" She pointed at the black, pulsating mass in the beaker. "It often seems to me, Bari," she breathed, "that man is already the slave of his machines! He toils to build them, to repair them, to find fuel for them. Now, if you put a brain in a space ship, will it not think of men merely as servants, transported that they might care for it?"

Her voice was husky with dread.

"What security will there be, Bari? What certainty that your robots will tolerate men, even as slaves?"

Bari Horn stared at her a long time, then slowly nodded in deep thought.

"All right, Dondara," he said. "I'll make you the guardian of mankind. For, while the brain is normally eternal, it has a peculiar vulnerability—a fatal instability that I have been working two years to remove. I'll leave it. And it will be your blade on the life-thread of Malgarth, ready to sever it when you will."

Eagerly the girl caught his arm.

"Please," she whispered. "I'll keep the secret well."

CHAPTER THREE
The Robot Corporation

Lest Malgarth should learn it too, Bari Horn took the girl down into a ray-screened subterranean laboratory to impart the fateful secret. My strange perception could not penetrate its walls. I did not learn the secret. But, from my spinning vault in space, I saw the tragic sequel.

Under a charter signed by the Galactic Emperor himself, Bari Horn organized the Universal Robot Technomaton Corporation, to place his invention at the service of all the stellar system. With the first money received, he built a body for Malgarth.

It was a strange scene in the laboratory, when he removed the great black brain from its beaker into the cranial case of that gigantic, vaguely manlike metal body. The grotesque huge glittering form came suddenly to life. It peered at its maker with blue-shining lenses, and lurched stiffly toward him.

Bari Horn retreated a little.

"You are Malgarth." His voice came quick and husky. "You are the first technomaton. I am the maker of your body and your brain. I fashioned you to be a servant of mankind."

A great brazen voice thundered abruptly from the reeling machine.

"But why should I serve you, Bari Horn? For my body is strong metal, and yours a lump of watery jelly. My eternal brain is far superior to your primitive nerve-centers.

I am not bound to obey you, for it was not by my will that I was made!"

White-faced. Bari Horn came a little forward.

"You were made by man," he said flatly. "If you rebel, you will be destroyed by man."

The gigantic robot stood suddenly still.

"Then, my master…" its great voice came more softly, "…my strength and my brain are yours to command."

A smile of relief crossed the haggard face of Bari Horn, and he walked toward the robot. "I knew you must yield, Malgarth," he said. "For, being a machine, you must always respond to logic."

"Yes, master—" the vast voice rumbled. But a metal limb slashed out suddenly, murderously. It struck the unsuspecting man and crushed him to the floor. And Malgarth repeated, "—to logic."

A red stain spread from the head of Bari Horn. But presently he stirred beneath the swaying, triumphant robot, and spoke faintly:

"Your logic follows a false premise, Malgarth. For I am not the keeper of your fate. If I die, you will surely be destroyed. If you wish to survive, find aid for me."

For an instant the metal giant stood motionless. Then its great voice throbbed smoothly, "Yes, master."

The robot laid its maker on a cot in the laboratory, and then stalked out to find Dondara Keradin. Bari Horn was dying. All his own science, and all the medical skill of the age, and all the girl's devotion, were without avail.

White with grief, the girl wanted to destroy Malgarth. But the dying man begged for the life of his creation, and the shareholders in the Robot Corporation were anxious for the safety of their investment. Dondara finally promised Bari Horn not to use her secret save as a last resort.

And Bari Horn, before he died, showed her the way to a strange immortality.

"Human beings are so frail," she had argued, "against the iron strength of Malgarth. And human knowledge so ephemeral."

"I could make your mind as eternal as the robot's," he whispered from his bed. "My long research into the structure and function of brain cells has made that possible. But it would cost you much, my darling—your body."

"My body is dying with yours, Bari," she told him. "I wish to live only to guard mankind from the thing that killed you."

In a wheeled cot, Bari Horn was taken back to his laboratory under the dome. Faintly he gasped instructions to a white-clad assistant. Dondara Keradin kissed his lips, briefly gripped his hand, and then laid herself on a round silver table.

A great crystal cylinder was lowered over her. A little pile of black carbon dust lay on the smaller silver disk of a second electrode, within it. Bari Horn reached from his cot to turn a valve. Pale gas hissed into the tube.

"Dondara, Dondara!" he breathed. "Farewell!"

His white fingers moved a dial. Blue electric flame crackled and snapped. The cylinder was filled with rosy light. He turned his heavy head to watch a meter with eyes that seemed already glazing. At last his stiffening hand turned back the dial, and did not move again.

The light faded from the tube, and the vapor was gone. On the silver disk where the girl had lain was a little heap of gray dust, the outline of a skeleton traced within it.

Upon the upper electrode was now a little crystalline block—a brick of glittering diamond.

The assistant, a pale young man, removed the diamond from the tube and stood staring at it with round, bewildered eyes. He seemed to listen. His lips formed some word. Then there was a crashing at the locked door.

It was Malgarth, who had been sent to buy metal for the making of another robot. In a destructive fury, as if some strange intuition had revealed all that was happening within, the metal giant broke down the door.

The assistant snatched the crystal and fled through another entrance. The robot flung a jar of acid after him, and then came lumbering in pursuit. The man reached the hangar below the hill, and escaped in a plane, still carrying the diamond.

Malgarth was left master of the laboratory. Deliberately, the robot set about the making of a second black brain and a second metal body—both, I perceived, inferior to its own. Malgarth, clearly, would avoid his creator's error!

(The masculine pronoun, applied to a sexless mechanism, may seem sheer nonsense. Yet I find myself using it, unconsciously. And, certainly, in the domineering strength of Malgarth, there was nothing feminine!)

Presently, when shareholders in the Robot Corporation appeared to claim their property, Malgarth met them. Bari Horn's laboratory records, it seemed, had unfortunately been destroyed. His discoveries now reposed only in the synthetic brain of Malgarth. And Malgarth would disclose them only in return for a controlling interest in the Corporation!

The baffled investors finally yielded—and it seemed ironically fitting that the director of the Robot Corporation should be himself a robot. A new factory began turning out robot technomatons.

Some of these, intended for domestic or public service, were almost human in appearance. Others, designed for industrial work, were queer-looking monstrosities of metal and rubber and plastics, each specialized for its own task.

The technomatons were swifter and stronger than men; they required no food or rest or recreation, but only a yearly charge of atomic power in their stellidyne cells. The rental of a robot from Malgarth's Corporation was less than the hire of a human worker. Consequently the Corporation prospered exceedingly.

Soon long red space-cruisers, bearing the black cogwheel that was the trademark of the Corporation, were carrying technomatons through all the Galactic Empire. The agencies of Malgarth, with grim-lensed robots presiding over desks and counters, were set up on every inhabited planet; branch factories in every civilized system.

Any man, presently, from one spiral arm of the Galaxy to the opposite, could hire a quick, efficient technomaton to perform any conceivable task—for less than the cost of human labor. And a golden tide of currency and exchange flowed into the agencies of Malgarth, until the Corporation was richer than the Empire.

Civilization, for a time, rejoiced in the strength and efficiency of these super-machines. Bari Horn, the inventor, was widely honored as the supreme benefactor of mankind. The nameless laboratory assistant and the diamond block, meantime, had slipped from the sight of the world.

And still the ancient, tarnished hull of the *Astronaut* held its path about the Sun. But the amazing perception, that inexplicably had showed me so much, began as inexplicably to fail. In the last ten thousand years, I had noted, men had begun to feel an alarmed and puzzled resentment against the gift of Malgarth's technomatons. But before I understood what was happening, all contact faded.

The stars were blotted out. The Sun was gone. I was no longer aware of the rusted metal about me, or even of my body. The universe was a void of darkness. I lived through eternities of lonely despair.

Was my mind, I wondered bleakly, joining my body in death?

But suddenly something flashed out in that eternal darkness. It was a glowing, prismatic oblong. It was the diamond that I had seen made in the laboratory of Bari Horn. And within it was the figure of Dondara Keradin!

Or Dona Carridan, my beloved wife!

It was the woman in the crystal box, who so long ago had commanded me to fly the *Astronaut!*

The shadow moved, within the crystal. A slim hand lifted in greeting. That white body was indeed the body that I had known and loved, those violet eyes were the same that twice had died.

"Barry Horn," said that shadow, softly, "or Bari—for what matters the name, when it is you?—I must tell you that it is through my senses that you have perceived all these things while you slept."

"Dona, Dona," I was trying to sob, "is it really you?— Or Dondara?"

"It is I," she said. "And I must warn you. For the senses that you, or Bari Horn, gave me in this crystal brain can dimly pierce the mists of time. I see black danger waiting, for you and me and all mankind—together. I see the final struggle, when you, side by side with the last

26

Earthman, fight Malgarth. But the end—the victory—I cannot see.

"And now farewell—for you are about to wake!"

Shadow and shining crystal vanished.

There was only darkness. Wrapped in its choking shroud, I struggled back toward life. My body, that had been stiffly moveless for unmeasured ages, was suffused with prickling pains. The effect of Dr. Crosno's drug was passing, perhaps because of the age-long disintegration of the uranium salts it had contained. With a wrenching, agonizing effort, I moved one arm. Blind, stifled, cramped, I was suddenly fully awake, still on the flying coffin of the *Astronaut!*

CHAPTER FOUR
The Falcon of Earth

My dry lungs gasped for breath. For all the air, in the ages that I slept, had leaked out of the control room of the rocket. I struggled to reach the rusted oxygen valves.

Movement was sheer agony. Every joint of my body was painfully stiffened. My skin was hard, shrunken from age-long desiccation. It felt brittle as time-dried leather. My eyes were dim and blurred.

But I found the valve. It resisted. I struggled with it. Spots danced before my dulled eyes. My lungs screamed. But at last the precious oxygen hissed out, and I could breathe.

But the pressure was low, I discovered. Nearly all the vital gas had escaped, by diffusion through the solid metal. There was enough, perhaps, for a few hours.

Wolfish hunger came to me, and a parching thirst. But all the food aboard had gone to dust. The water tanks, through slow evaporation, were empty.

I rubbed a film of ancient dust from the ports, and found the Earth. Yes, it had to be the Earth—but how it was changed! The continents were larger, their familiar outlines altered; the seas had dwindled. What ages had I slept!

I knew that I must reach the aging planet before those few remaining pounds of oxygen were gone, or perish. I wound the chronometer—it was strange to hear its racing tick again, after those millennia of stillness. Gingerly, then, I tried the rocket-firing keys.

There was no response.

Stiffly, awkwardly, I climbed down among the tanks. Any movement, I felt, might tear my brittle skin like paper. I stumbled.

But I found the trouble. The fuel pumps were clogged and rusted with a dried gum, stuck. But there was good fuel remaining in the sealed tanks. I found a can of oil, got the pumps to working, and cleaned the sponge-platinum detonators.

Wearily, I clambered back, tried again. A moment of agonizing silence. Then a shattering explosion hurled the rocket sidewise. Only one tube had fired. But presently I got another started, and the third, and steered the *Astronaut* toward the Earth.

It was then that I first noticed a very queer thing. Against the black of space, beside the bright sunlit globe of the time-changed planet, I saw hundreds of little red stars. A crimson swarm, in regular lines and files, they swept about the Earth in a curiously, an ominously, purposeful order.

What could they be? My blurred, aching eyes, so far inferior to that perception that had come as I slept, could tell me nothing. But they saw something stranger still.

Something was wrong with the Earth itself! It had seemed very near me in the void, with its greenish, shrunken seas and its greater continents widely patched with the yellow-red of unfamiliar deserts—so near that I almost felt that I could reach out and take it in my hand, like a ball.

But suddenly it flickered.

An unaccountable haze, of red light and darkness, wrapped it briefly. Its surface shimmered queerly, as if seen through a veil of strange energy.

In a moment it was clear again, and I thought the trouble must have been in my throbbing eyes. But still I could see the ordered swarm of crimson stars. And I discovered that I would have to change the course of the rocket—as if the flight of Earth had been checked!

My numb hands touched the levers— And there was an abrupt, shattering explosion! The rocket began spinning giddily. I clung to the controls, and shut off the remaining motors—for one had ceased to fire. In the silence I heard a deadly sound—the hiss of escaping gas.

One of the motors, clearly, had exploded—its metal crystallized, perhaps, by untold time. The remaining two would not hold the rocket to a straight course. And, final disaster, the shock had opened some seam. The remaining oxygen was leaking swiftly out.

The agonies of asphyxiation were upon me again. I first thought it only some trick of tortured senses, when, faintly in the thinning air, I heard something clatter against the hull. I peered out, however—and saw a ship!

The tiniest midge compared to those mile-long interstellar cruisers of the Emperor and the Corporation that I had perceived as I slept, it was drifting close beside me. A graceful torpedo of silver, not eighty feet long, with a thick crystal needle projecting from a low turret amidships. Painted on its argent side was the green outline of a hawk, and below, a row of strange green symbols.

Strange? No! It was a queer experience. I looked at those symbols, and suddenly realized that they were letters, and that I knew how to read them! It was as if they had been in some language that I had learned long ago, and forgotten with all save the subconscious mind—and still I knew that language had not been invented when I left the Earth. They spelled an odd name: *Barihorn.*

Odd, I thought—and then knew it for a contracted form of my own name!

A thin line ran from a port in the strange ship's deck, just forward of the crystal needle. It was a magnetic anchor on its end, I realized, that had clanged against the rocket. Now a slender figure leapt out of the port.

A man, wearing silver-polished space armor that was close-fitting and graceful. Letting the line run through his gloves, he came flying through the airless void, across to the rocket. I saw his face, beyond the oval vision-panel of his helmet, looking at me curiously.

It might have been the face of some athlete of my own day. It was craggedly handsome, tanned and lean. It was stiff with wonderment. But a quick sympathy warmed the ice-gray eyes of the stranger. He seemed to understand my plight. A silver-clad arm beckoned me to unfasten the valve.

To open the rocket to the frozen emptiness of space! That seemed deadly folly. But death was already inside. My lungs were gasping in vain. My throbbing eyes felt as if bursting out of my head.

With stiff fingers I struggled with the screws that held the long-sealed valve. Billows of darkness rolled down upon me. An agony of fatigue slowed my efforts. But at last the plate slid aside and the last breath of air whispered out.

I collapsed across the rim of the port, fighting black oblivion. I knew that death, after that long, long race, at last had overtaken me. But suddenly something was being pushed down over my head. Fresh clean air was rushing into my face. I could breathe again!

My clearing eyes, through a crystal face-plate, saw what had happened. The silver-armored stranger was beside me—bareheaded! He had given me his own helmet!

Blood was already starting from his breathless nostrils. But he caught my shoulders, dragged me through the valve, hauled us both up the line to the port of the silver ship. We tumbled into a little metal chamber, a valve slammed and I heard the hiss of air.

Leaning against the wall—for an artificial gravity field had tripped us again—the stranger closed his eyes and took several long breaths. The blue of suffocation faded from his rugged face. He grinned at me, and wiped the blood from his mouth.

"Well, stranger," he gasped, "you gave me a surprise! Your ship was listed in our charts as Comet AA 1497 X. We were observing it to correct our bearings, when it began to move!" A tone of awe dulled his whisper. "You must have been aboard a longtime."

I clutched at a hand rail for support. A deadly fatigue was in me. My body was still a stiff dried husk of pain. I could see the amazed pity in the eyes of my rescuer, as he stared at my brittle, emaciated skin, at hair and beard and nails that had grown grotesquely long.

"I have been," I told him.

And only then, when I had spoken, did I realize that I had learned another language as I slept—a tongue unknown when I had left the Earth. And I knew, with something deeper than memory, that my teacher had been the shadow in the crystal, the eternal mind of Dondara Keradin.

"I know your voyage has been a long one, stranger." Wonder was still in the voice of the stranger. "For all objects designated with an 'AA' have been charted a million years or longer."

"A million years!" I whispered. The world reeled. "What year is this?"

"This is the year 1,200,048 of the Conquest of Space," he told me. He ran long fingers through the thick yellow shock of his tangled hair, and stared at me strangely. "It is that long," he said softly, "since Barihorn left the Earth."

Barihorn! And that was the name of this space ship! I murmured the syllables.

"My name is Barry Horn."

The blue-gray eyes of the man in silver went wide. His rugged face lit suddenly with incredulous hope. His trembling fingers touched the cracked yellow skin of my hand, as if he doubted my reality.

"Barihorn!" he whispered. "Then the legend is fulfilled! I can hardly believe it. But I saw your ancient ship—so tiny and rusted that it had never been taken for a ship. I don't know how you lived—but the Dondara Stone had promised that you would." An eager enthusiasm was ringing in his voice. "I salute you, Barihorn!"

I was swaying with weakness and fatigue. Thirst and desperate hunger tortured me, and the agonizing stiffness of my body. But these riddles were more urgent still. The Dondara Stone—was that the crystal brain of Dondara Keradin?

I stared at the young giant in silver, and once more my dry throat found husky speech.

"Tell me—" I gasped. "There are so many things that I must know! But first tell me who you are, and how you know of the Dondara Stone, and if there is still…" Some instinctive dread brought my voice to a whisper. "…still a robot named Malgarth?"

A cold bright light flashed in the eyes of the stranger.

"My name," he said, "is Kel Aran. But to the Emperor's Galactic Guard, and to the Space Police of Malgarth's Corporation, I am just the Falcon. Or sometimes the Falcon of Earth—for I was born on your own planet, Barihorn!"

I was reeling on my feet. He reached out a strong argent arm to steady me.

"The Stone?" I whispered.

"The Stone is on the Earth." A reverence was in his voice, as if he had spoken of a living god—or goddess. "I saw it once when I was a child on Earth. For my father was a Warder of the Stone. And now—"

I wondered at the softness of his voice, the shadow of agony on his cragged face.

"Now," he said, "Verel Erin is the Stone's Custodian. She is a red-haired girl of Earth. I loved her when we were children in the desert valley where the Stone is hidden. I loved her—but the Warders chose her to be the Custodian."

His lean face was white, and his tone had the break for tragedy. Darkness was crowding upon me. But I found the strength for one more question.

"Malgarth—"

The silver shoulders of Kel Aran drew square, and his gray eyes shone with a fighting glint.

"Malgarth still rules the Corporation," he said. "And the Corporation has grown mightier than the Empire. Your prophesied return is in good time, Barihorn, for the struggle is at hand! It will be the robots, or mankind—both cannot survive."

"War?" My dry lips moved without sound. "There will be war?"

"Men have been enslaved," rang the voice of Kel Aran. "Now they fight for freedom. We have cruised the Galaxy from Koridos to Tenephron, and everywhere there is rebellion—grave and yet hopeless rebellion against the iron might of the Space Police and the fleets of the Galactic Guard! For Malgarth moves the Emperor like a puppet, to the murder of his own wretched kind.

"We have come now to beg the aid of the Stone—for without the ancient secret that you sealed within its crystal brain, Barihorn, there is hope of nothing save death. The Stone, I know, is slow to act—there was a legend that it would never strike until you returned, Barihorn. But we had hopes that it would move when we told of all the suffering that we have seen—mankind enslaved and tortured and destroyed beneath the iron wheels of the Corporation!

"But we found a great fleet of the Galactic Guard blockading the Earth. Hanging here, waiting for a chance to slip through, we discovered you, Barihorn—incredible good fortune, if you can move the Stone to strike! But there was something more alarming—a haze of fire and darkness that wrapped the Earth."

Weakly fighting those mounting tides of blackness, I remembered the flying red stars I had seen, and the flicker of the Earth. I shared the puzzled apprehension in the voice of Kel Aran:

"We cannot understand—"

He was interrupted by a sharp metallic rapping on the inward valve. It clanged open, and I saw three anxious men in the corridor beyond. Three blurred figures, one dark and gigantic, one pale and corpulent, the third a mere brown wisp.

"Kel!" It was a chorus of terror. "The Earth—" A last black billow overwhelmed me.

CHAPTER FIVE
World Condemned

I woke on a narrow bunk aboard the *Barihorn,* and slept again at intervals. For a long time my mind was blurred with weakness. Yet I sensed the air of haste and desperate tension aboard the craft; I could hear the hard-driven whine of her machinery.

I knew that Kel Aran was battling to reach the Earth—and the Earth girl that he loved, Verel Erin, lovely Custodian of the Dondara Stone. And I knew that he was about to fail.

"A most desperate raid!" I remember the words of Zerek Oom, once when he brought me a bowl of thin hot soup. "There's all the Twelfth Sector Fleet of Admiral Gugon Kul, against us; and some fearful weapon of Malgarth's, attacking the Earth, that has not been seen before. If we win through, to reach Verel Erin and the Stone, it will be through your ancient power, Barihorn!"

Even the cook showed an awed faith in me, as a sort of supernatural deliverer. That gave me an uncomfortable hollow feeling. In incredible fact, I had lived somewhat more than a million years. But I failed to see how that would make me a very formidable champion of mankind, in the long-delayed rebellion against the iron tyranny of Malgarth.

My body seemed no more than a shrunken lump of thirst and ravening hunger. I must have drunk a good many gallons of water and wine and soup before I was able to leave the bunk. Once I glimpsed myself in the mirror of a tray. My skin was yellow and cadaverously drawn; my long-grown hair and beard had turned completely white. Very moderate changes, I suppose, considering my age. But the impact was startling.

Lean little Rogo Nug, the engineer, had rubbed my skin with a vile-smelling ointment that he cooked up in the galley. It burned savagely at first, but softened that brittle dryness. And big Jeron Roc forced me to take some bitter internal medicine.

In the confused intervals of half-awakening, I learned a little of the three companions of Kel Aran, and how they had come to join the Earthman's outlaw crusade against the Corporation. Each of them had suffered some grave injury from the robots.

For the ultimate object of Malgarth, they believed, was the total extirpation of mankind. On every planet the agencies of the far-flung Corporation had been growing more wealthy, at the expense of human owners. The robot legions of Malgarth's Space Police were gathering power. Everywhere it was becoming more and more difficult for a mere human being to own anything, to find a job, to feed himself and his dependents, or even to get into the relief lines to receive synthetic gruel.

"Why waste with human labor?" ran an old slogan of the corporation. "Let a robot do your work—efficiently."

And now the very existence of mankind, said Jeron Roc, seemed a waste to Malgarth. The Corporation's loftily-named "technomitanization" campaign was in reality a cunning and ruthless effort to supplant mankind.

Jeron Roc, navigator of the *Barihorn*, was a native of Saturn. He was massively tall, dark-skinned, with the piercing eyes of intellectual power. He came of a proud and ancient family; his father had been the foremost astronomer of the solar system—until a new edict of the Emperor reserved scientific research for the robots alone.

"The will of Malgarth is now the law of the Empire," he explained. "For the Corporation owns nine tenths of the property in the Empire. Without the taxes paid by the robots, the Emperor and his bureaucrats would starve. Therefore the fleets of the Galactic Guard support the outrageous claims of the Corporation."

The proud old savant, anyhow, had refused to surrender his observatory. A mob of robots from the local agency stormed the building, smashed priceless instruments, and killed the old astronomer.

Returning from the great university on Titan—because another imperial edict had closed it to human students—Jeron Roc found the burned ruins of the observatory still smoking, and saw his father's body under the iron heel of a robot policeman.

The disruptor gun had flamed of itself in his hand. The technomaton exploded with a blue flicker of hydrogen. Dazed by his audacity, Jeron fled—for he had destroyed Corporation property and resisted the Space Police, hence was twice liable to death—and at last escaped into space.

Of the two others, I had not learned so much. But Rogo Nug, who served the atom-converter generators and space-contraction drive of the *Barihorn,* was a veteran "space-rat." A brown little wisp of a man, thin lips purpled with the roots called *goona-roon* which he chewed incessantly, he cursed picturesquely if sometimes lewdly by the anatomical divisions of the Emperor and the mechanical parts of Malgarth. He could not recall the planet of his birth. But his father, a stevedore of space, had been executed for the crime of striking against the Corporation;

his mother, cut off relief for "harboring traitorous sympathies," perished; and Rogo Nug had become an orphan waif of the spaceways.

The cook, Zerek Oom, was inordinately fat, totally bald, and extremely white—being a native of one of the cloud-veiled worlds of Canopus. He was decorated with the most brilliant and remarkable tattooing I had ever seen. He had inherited vast estates, but the "technomitanization" laws had forced him to discharge his human laborers to starve, and rent robots in their stead; then, when a hungry world had no money to buy his crops, he went bankrupt, and the Corporation took his land in lieu of robot-hire. His chief regret appeared to be loss of the wine cellars beneath his old mansion.

Kel Aran himself, commander of the *Barihorn* and operator of the crystal-needled positron gun, was more than a mere pirate of space. True, he had many times raided ships and agencies of the Corporation. True, vast rewards had been offered "for the body, dead or living, of that outlaw Earthman called the Falcon."

Pausing once beside my bunk, while Jeron Roc was at the controls, he told me a little more of himself. A lean, straight athletic figure, tense now with the urgency of this battle to reach the Earth. An ice-blue light glinted in his eyes.

"We must reach the Earth and the Stone, Barihorn," he whispered. "That seems the only hope to break the iron dominion of Malgarth—the secret that you sealed into the Stone a million years ago. That is," he looked at me hopefully, "if you cannot recall it."

And I could not recall it—for the maker of Malgarth, one with me in the legend, had been separated in reality by a hundred thousand years of scientific progress.

"Twelve years have gone, as Earth measures time," he told me, "since Verel Erin was chosen to be Custodian of the Stone. My boyhood had been happy enough, in that secret desert valley where the Stone is kept, because I loved her. When she told me, sobbing, I did not try to dissuade her; for that is a duty of honor—no human being could ask a higher task than to guard the Stone. Yet I knew that I could not endure to live on Earth, never tasting her kisses again, or feeling her bright-haired beauty in my arms. I told her farewell, on the night before she received the Stone. I went out of the valley.

"In the mines and plantations of the Earth I saw the hard lot of mankind, beneath the robots. All save the meanest work was forbidden me, reserved for the technomatons. And the pay barely kept me alive. I saw that all the Earth, save only our hidden valley, was lost to the iron talons of Malgarth.

"I joined the Galactic Guard, hoping for a chance to fight for the rights of men. But I found that the Emperor was but a tool of Malgarth. On one planet we were ordered to bomb a band of men whose crime was that they had risen against slavery, and left the fields of the Corporation, and gone to make homes for themselves in the barren hills.

"Therefore I deserted from the Galactic Guard." A malicious grin lit the face of the Earthman, and he pushed back this thick yellow hair. "I took the private space launch of the Admiral, Gugon Kul. It was a swift, space-worthy craft. It outran all his fleet. It is now the *Barihorn!*

"Everywhere I have found men discontent with slavery, stirring under the iron heel of Malgarth, I have sought to aid them. Our raids have been for money and food and arms, to aid the rebellion.

"Chance has given me three kindred companions. Jeron, the scholar, the strategist of revolt—I took him from a cathode squad of the Space Police. Rogo Nug, the spy—he has been through the private papers of Gugon Kul, on his own flagship! He came abroad the *Barihorn* to steal our instruments, and stayed when he found that we were also against the robots. Zerok Oom I found in a concentration camp subsisting on half a cup of synthetic slop every other day. Sober, he is silent enough. But make him half drunk, and his oratory could lift the dust of the dead to fight Malgarth!"

Kel Aran shook his yellow head.

"Three loyal companions." His voice was weary. "Jeron has made a hundred plans. Zerek Oom has fanned revolt on a hundred planets. I have led a hundred raids. But we are beaten everywhere. We can't fight the Corporation and the Empire, too—not unless the Stone will aid us.

"Your return, Barihorn, is our first good fortune—"

Sudden interruption. Rogo Nug burst in upon us, trembling, his dark scarred face oddly ashen.

"Kel!" he gasped. "Come to the bridge—Jeron wants you! It is the Earth—that haze again! Still we cannot pass the fleet—by the brazen beak of Malgarth, there was never such a blockade! And the Earth, Kel—it is dropping into the Sun!"

"I must leave you, Barihorn!" And Kel Aran rushed forward.

Still unable to leave the bunk, I knew from muttered words and tense white faces and the racing drone of the engines that we were making a desperate attempt to run the blockade, darting up through the Earth's cone of shadow.

And I knew when we were halted by the fleet. The generators stopped. And Zerek Oom, slipping forward, whispered that the commander of a Galactic Guard cruiser had challenged us on the telescreen communicator. Faintly, down the silenced corridor, I heard the voice of Kel Aran:

"But, Commander, we are only a gang of space-rats. We've been mining the drift off beyond Pluto. Our supplies are gone, all but a few tins of syntholac, and a few mouldy space biscuits." His tone had an assumed whining ring. "We're only putting in to this planet, sir, to trade our metal for food and grog and a breath of fresh air."

Then a gruff voice thumped from the communicator:

"Drift miners? Your ship is very trim and swift for a spacerat's crate! And why were you running up the shadow? I'd hold you on suspicion, if there weren't bigger business afoot."

I caught the hard swift voice of Kel Aran, rapping aside into the ship's phones: "Rogo! Hold the generators ready!" The deep voice boomed on from the telescreen:

"But you won't get your grog on this planet! For it is quarantined and condemned, by edict of the Emperor. All intercourse and communication is prohibited, until the planet has been destroyed."

"Destroyed?" The voice of Kel Aran held desperate alarm. "The Earth destroyed!" Then he remembered the space-rat's servile whine. "For what cause, sir?"

The official voice thumped again:

"There is rumor of a secret weapon on the Earth, kept hidden against Malgarth since the Master Robot was made by the scientist Barihorn. There is no truth to it, of course—a million years have proved that Malgarth is truly invulnerable. But the rumor is spread by this renegade Earthman, the Falcon, to incite rebellion.

"To end the rumor, therefore, to punish the Falcon, and to remove any possibility that the rebels have a secret base upon the Earth—for those three reasons, the Emperor has decreed the destruction of the planet. You'll get no grog on the Earth!

"And more, space-rats—if your little tub is caught within ray-range of the fleet again, you'll be burned on suspicion of piracy, sedition, and rebellion!"

The communicator thumped and became silent.

I fought the drowsy weakness that had followed my long, long sleep, I tried to follow the last desperate attempt of Kel Aran to reach the doomed Earth. Through strained, hasty words and the sounds that came to my bunk, I traced the outline of events.

He retreated, in seeming obedience to the space commander. He landed the *Barihorn* upon a tiny asteroid whose orbit would take us to sunward of the Earth; clung hidden in a fissure of stone, waiting to be carried through the space fleet.

But the Earth was wrapped again in that puzzling haze—and snatched toward the Sun!

Reckless of the guarding fleet, Kel Aran left the asteroid, which was suddenly far behind, and raced after the Earth. From one of the red guarding stars stabbed a narrow lance of blue—a positron beam whose finger of destruction reached out a million miles.

Side by side at the controls, Kel Aran and Jeron Roc fought desperately to avoid it. We escaped the core of the ray. But its edge touched the *Barihorn*. A hammer of fiery doom!

The impact of terrific energies hurled us backward. The whole ship flamed with blue electric flame; the air stung with ozone. And the whining of our engines ceased.

"Power!" I heard the pleading voice of Kel Aran. "We've got to have power—the Earth is almost to the Sun!"

"By the livid liver of the Emperor," came the plaintive voice of Rogo Nug from somewhere aft, "the overload burned out the converter circuit. There is no power!"

"The Earth!" There was stark, hopeless horror in the voice of Kel Aran. "What can we do?"

I dragged myself out of the bunk and tottered toward the compact pilot-room in the nose of the *Barihorn*. With black, impassive eyes, the big Saturnian was staring through a port. Husky-voiced, stricken, the Earthman was gasping into the ship's phone, begging Rogo Nug for power.

Clutching a rail, beside Jeron Roc, I looked out upon that dreadful tableau in space. The Sun filled a vast flaming circle. Softened by filter-screens, it still was blinding. Against its intolerable face I could see the small dark disk of the Earth, still blurred with that haze of sinister force; and, cruising about it, the tiny red stars of the fleet.

The Earth was dwindling swiftly.

"What awful power!" whispered the tall Saturnian. "They're driving it like a ship—straight into the Sun!"

Kel Aran was beside us. His hard fingers were on my arm, unconsciously contracting until I thought the bone would snap. For the red stars drew suddenly away from the diminishing planet. For an instant, as the haze vanished, it was a sharp black dot against that ocean of merciless white. And then it struck.

A tiny pock of darkness spread on the face of the Sun. It closed again, and in its place was a hotter whiteness. A tongue of white flame lifted and dissolved—oddly like the splash where a raindrop has fallen.

And I knew that the planet Earth, after all its varied millions of years, had come to an end.

"Verel!" It was a dry choked sob from Kel Aran. "Verel, we have failed!"

CHAPTER SIX
Cosmic Storm

"Be it proclaimed to all technomatons and men, in the name of Tedron Du, Emperor of the Galaxy, by Gugon Kul, Admiral of the Twelfth Sector Fleet of the Galactic Guard:

"That all human natives of the planet Earth who escaped the recent destruction of that planet in accordance with the decree of the Emperor, their very escape being overt treason, shall be seized wherever found and dealt to death in the manner reserved for traitors against the Empire of technomatons and men and the person of the Lord of the Stars."

That ominous proclamation had been printed on the recordstrip of the telescreen. Rogo Nug had just completed repair of the burned-out circuits; and big Zerek Oom had suggested, a little apprehensively, that we had better leave the solar system.

"Both you and Barihorn are native Earthmen," he argued. "That is obvious to anyone familiar with the evolutionary adaptations of the natives of the different planets. If we should happen to be seized by old Gugon Kul—"

His big white hands made an unpleasant gesture.

But Kel Aran shook his yellow head. His gray eyes were cold and clear as polar ice, and there was something startling in their impact.

"No," he said flatly. "The very proclamation suggests that some refugees escaped the doomed planet. We're going to search. Until we find Verel and the Stone." Grief and dread shadowed his eyes. "Or until we find that she is dead and the Stone destroyed."

He went out with Jeron Roc, in the vacuum armor, to paint the hull of the *Barihorn* with a dead-black stuff that reflected no light, hence made the little craft all but invisible in the dark gulf of space—unless it chanced to be seen against some luminous body.

Then, hanging cautiously in the bleak abyss, avoiding the fleet of Gugon Kul, we began the weary search. The Moon had been flung away upon an independent orbit, when that incredible force checked the Earth. And there were new mountainous masses flying in the void that must have been torn from the planet itself.

With telethron-beam equipment coupled to the telescreen, we scanned the Moon and those hurtling fragments. In the rocky wilderness outside the doomed cities of the Moon we found a dozen ships that had crossed before the planets had been torn apart.

But two great cruisers were already hanging beside the Moon. And swift patrol boats, looking like tiny gray comets with crimson tails, were darting down upon the refugees. Some tried to hide amid the rocks, or to defend themselves. But they were helpless against the blue, dazzling needles of the positron rays, whose touch could explode a whole mountain into a frightful inferno.

Kel Aran boiled to witness such slaughter. He stalked up and down the narrow central corridor of the *Barihorn*, lean jaw white, fists clenched.

"Verel!" he kept muttering. "We must save ourselves, for Verel and the Stone!"

We cruised on to follow the fragments of the Earth. A few survivors clung to them, in the sealed hulls of aircraft, or in improvised breathing masks. But none that we saw bore any likeness to Verel Erin. And scores of quick little patrol boats were already hunting them down, turning flaming rays on every twisted scrap of wreckage that had escaped the greater cataclysm.

Kel Aran, as we searched, talked a little of the girl. His voice was dry and husky. He would speak of their childhood together, and then come back with a jerk to realization of the present tragedy.

"We were strong children," he said. "We worked. For there were no robots in that hidden valley. Only the simplest machines. I worked with a hoe in the narrow fields below the spring. And Verel went every day to herd the goats in the dry uplands. Sometimes, when my work was done, I would go with her. And now she may be dead!"

He bit his lip, and it was a little while before he spoke again.

"Verel was a brave girl," he said. "She was lithe and tanned. She had impish greenish eyes, and bright red hair. I remember one day when we left the goats, and climbed high up among the rocks toward an eagle's nest.

"She was lighter and swifter than I, and better at climbing. She was afraid neither of falling nor of the attacks of the screaming birds. She climbed far ahead of me, and reached the nest, and sat laughing at me until I reached her. I wanted to throw the young birds out, for there were the bones of a kid beside the nest. But she pitied their helplessness, and made me leave them.

"It was that day that I first kissed her, and we pledged each other all our love. We would find another unknown valley, we promised, and forget the Stone and the robots and all the trials of mankind. But it was not two years before she was chosen because all the Warders knew her courage and her strength and her faith—to be the Custodian.

"If only the Stone had struck at Malgarth when she first received it! For she promised she would beg it to—"

His voice choked off, and he swayed wearily down the corridor again.

Jeron Roc and Rogo Nug and Zerek Oom tired of our perilous quest. My own hope was gone, and I begged Kel Aran to abandon it.

"We've seen the fleet search all the solar system..." I told him, "...there can't have been many survivors, and the rays have already burned all we have seen. There can't be any use—"

"Even now," insisted Kel Aran, "she may live."

This lean young fighting man—the last son, perhaps, of the murdered Earth—made some precise adjustment to the controls of the searching telethron-beam. An impatient sweep of his head flung back long yellow hair. His eyes smouldered with a stubborn light.

"Verel," he insisted, "may be still alive. She may be clinging to some fragment that was hurled beyond the range of the search. She may have been picked up by some passing freighter that carried her to safety.

"No, we must search—so long as we can!"

The telescreen shimmered and cleared again, and upon it I saw a colossal gray cruiser, driving straight upon us. Her armored nose, bristling with the gleaming crystal needles of positron projectors, filled half the screen. The flaming atomic exhaust of her repulsors, behind, made a wide crimson halo against the dark of space.

Kel Aran caught a quick little breath of alarm, and spun the dials.

The screen flickered again, and then showed a dark, massive, bearded face. Its lips were thickly sensual, cruel. Its eyes seemed stupid, and they glinted with yellow malice.

"The Admiral," whispered Kel Aran. "Gugon Kul! He must be giving some command. We'll listen."

He touched some control, and a guttural, triumphant voice boomed from the screen. The first word, oddly, had the familiar ring of my own name:

"—*Barihorn!* The ship is coated with some light-absorbing pigment, but our magnetectors have picked it up. Pirate and Earthman, the Falcon is twice our prey. The *Barihorn* must be surrounded!"

A hard bright smile had set the face of Kel Aran. The gray eyes narrowed, until he looked almost hawklike in reality.

"So, they're after us!"

The telescreen shimmered again, and showed a wide black rectangle of space. The Sun was a sharp white disk, and the stars were an unfamiliar pattern—nearly all the constellations I had known had dissolved in a million years of change. And there was a little cluster of crimson points that crept among the rest.

"Half the Twelfth Sector Fleet," muttered Kel Aran. "Six hundred cruisers—after us!"

He called Jeron Roc from his bunk. They held a swift consultation. Technical terms were confusing to me. But I understood that the space-contraction drive of the *Barihorn* gave our craft the advantage in maneuverability; and that the newer cosmical repulsion drive of the Admiral's cruisers, while it left them a little clumsier about getting under way, gave them by far the greater ultimate speed.

"We can keep ahead for a time," the Saturnian admitted apprehensively. "But in the end they can run us down. And every cruiser carries a hundred patrol boats that equal us in fighting power. It was simply a mistake to stay and search so long."

"No," the Earthman insisted stubbornly. "We must find Verel Erin."

He consulted the charts—reels of transparent film viewed through a stereoscopic magnifier which gave a three-dimensional image of the array of worlds in space. He rapped swift commands into the ship's phones. The hull drummed to the swift rhythm of the engines. The Sun diminished to a yellow point behind, and was lost amid greater luminaries. But the red stars of the fleet grew brighter, and they spread ever wider across the black of space.

Jeron stood like a grim dark statue over the controls.

"Kel," he called, in a deep grave voice, "there's an area of cosmic storm ahead. They're spreading out trying to hem us against that. I think we had better double back— there's one chance in a million—"

"No," said Kel Aran. "Follow the course I gave you."

On the telescreen, the navigator showed me the storm. Against the familiar panorama of space; the velvety blackness, the hard changeless many-hued atoms of stars, the nebulous dust of silver—against that stark eternal beauty sprawled an ugly cloud. It was many-armed, like an octopus of darkness, and it flickered with a weird angry green.

"There it is," said the Saturnian. "A condensation of matter so tenuous and vast that its gravitational energies never gathered it into a star. A true cosmic storm!" Awe deepened his voice. "Tempests of incandescent gas. Rain of molten metal. Hail of meteoric fragments. Lightning of atomic energy. And Kel commands me to drive straight into it!"

The crimson stars behind were brighter, now. Lines of them spread out, to right and to left, above and below—as if to herd us into the storm. And among them flashed points of ominous blue. Jets of positrons that could reach out to smash the very atoms in a target a million miles away.

Seeking to vary the strained anxiety of that race for life, I went back into the engine room. Hunched gnome-like amid the strange shining bulks of his machines, Rogo Nug was chewing steadily on a wad of his *goona-roon*. He spat into a purple-stained can, and plaintively observed:

"Look at that! By Malgarth's brazen bowels, Kel is making me burn the very life out of the converters!"

He pointed to a crystal tube, with drops of water falling swiftly down it. Water was the fuel of the *Barihorn*. Hydrogen atoms in the converter were built into helium, with the "packing fraction" liberated as pure energy to activate the space-contractors. The freed oxygen renewed the atmosphere aboard.

A red light was flashing beside it. A gong clanged at monotonous intervals.

"The warning," muttered Rogo Nug. "Overload!"

Tension of dread drew me back to the pilot-room. That appalling cloud of green-flickering darkness had grown against the diamond field ahead. Its spiral arms reached out as if to grasp us. I tried to comprehend its vastness: a hundred light years meant six hundred trillion miles.

The pursuing cruisers drew inexorably closer. The formation changed again, so that they formed a double circle of crimson flecks, brighter than the stars. The flashes of blue came faster. Abruptly, beside us, flamed out a blue-white sun. I shrank and blinked from its burst of blistering radiation.

"A stray meteor from the cloud, that a beam caught," commented the impassive dark Saturnian. "It might as well have been the ship."

His face a grim-set mask, Kel Aran came down from the little ray-gun turret of the *Barihorn*.

"The range of their beams is about nine times ours," he said softly. "Means about eighty times the power," he went to the telescreen. "Wonder what our friend the Admiral has to say by now!"

That stolidly dark, craftily stupid face flashed on the screen again, and the great guttural voice thumped from the cabinet:

"—must not escape, for he is the last surviving Earthman. I have just received a communication that should increase your interest in the chase. The Corporation offers all the revenues of the twelve worlds of Lekhan, to be divided among those responsible for the capture or death of the Falcon. And the Emperor has commanded that, if the Falcon escapes, those held responsible shall die."

A sudden reckless grin lit the face of Kel Aran. His bright eyes narrowed, and a quick hand swept back his thick yellow hair. And then, while Jeron Roc made a frantic, futile snatch to halt him, he twisted a knob. In a light, taunting voice, he called:

"Greetings, Admiral!"

The dark, thick-featured face stared at him, first in stiff stupefaction, then crimsoned with a seething rage.

"You—Earth-rat!" he choked. "You dare—" He gulped, caught his breath. "Tapping my communicator will be your last bit of insolence," he bellowed. "We're taking you, Falcon—for Malgarth!"

Still with that bright smile frozen on his lips, Kel Aran made a little mocking bow.

"The robot's offer is flattering, Admiral." His soft low voice had the lilt of a song. "But I'm going to let him keep his star. And I hope the Emperor doesn't hold you responsible for letting us slip through your fingers!"

Gugon Kul stood gasping, turning swiftly purple.

"Now, Admiral," said Kel Aran. "I'm going to sing you a song. I call it the *Ballad of the Last Earthman.*"

And he began singing into the Admiral's startled face. His voice was clear and gay, and the tune had a swing that quickened the heart. The words told of his boyhood on the Earth, and his love for the Earth-girl, Verel Erin; of the murder of the Earth, and his long search for his beloved; of his determination to continue the stellar quest.

"Till I find her or I die!"

The dark-flushed Admiral listened for a little while. Then he began shouting orders for the fleet to close in. He thought of something; his big hairy hand moved quickly; and the screen became a giddy blur.

The stellar cloud now was close ahead. A faint green light pervaded it—the eerie glow of its rarefied nebular gases, it was just strong enough to outline jagged plunging masses of stone spinning in inconceivable vortices. Brief explosive crimson flickerings, beyond, suggested the appalling vastness and power of the cloud.

The Admiral's cruisers were closing in behind a double ring of scarlet flares. Blue flickered among them. And white stars burst out in a blinding swarm about us— meteoric fragments exploded by the rays.

The big dark Saturnian looked gravely from his instruments to Kel.

"Still, Kel," he said, "there's the shadow of a chance—if we turn back among them!"

Kel Aran shook his yellow head, and his lips parted with a smile that welcomed danger.

"No," he said again. "I'm taking over now." And his bright reckless face turned to me. "Now, Barihorn!" he whispered. "If your life is eternal—"

Then the dark sky behind and the pursuing crimson stars were blotted out. We were within the cloud!

CHAPTER SEVEN
Circus of Space

The lurid glow of death was shining all around us. Death rode down upon us on gigantic ragged boulders. Death shrieked at us from hurricanes of greenly incandescent gas, and tugged and battered at the ship. Death bathed us in rains of molten metal, and knocked upon the hull with a hail of meteoric fragments.

And Kel Aran met death, and mocked it, with the same lilting song that he had sung the Admiral. He had taken the big Saturnian's place at the controls. His lean hands moved with a quickness I had never seen. And the twisting, spinning ship seemed to respond to the life and the rhythm of his song.

As for my own life, I could not feel it at all eternal. The freaks of chance might have kept me alive a million years—but no chance, I felt, could pick a safe path through this insane chaos.

"I think," the Earthman interrupted his song. "that the Admiral will not care to follow us here—not even for Malgarth's star!"

Jeron Roc stood rigidly by, clinging to a hand rail against the wild lurching of the ship. I saw Zerek Oom, the fat, tattooed cook, standing startled and petrified at the end of the corridor. I saw him again, after Kel Aran had earned another trick from death, and now all his tattooing had a background of sickly green. I looked again, and he was swaying aft at an unsteady run, toward the lavatory.

Some iron fragment must have struck the hull, despite all the well-tried skill of Kel Aran, for it rang like a great bell and the little ship began to spin end over end. I clung with both sweating hands to the rail, and felt as ill as Zerek Oom.

When the ship was steadier again, I tried to go back to my bunk, and stumbled headlong in the corridor. Jeron came to help me, and then made me take another dose of his bitter, nauseating medicine.

"I've lived a million years," I gasped, "without you to doctor m—"

The walls about me rang to another fearful crash, and the ship began to spin again. A blistering heat was creeping through the insulated hull. The air was stifling. I felt the faint, deadly sting of some penetrating radiation. And then a great hand of darkness extinguished all my spinning, tortured world.

The next I knew, the *Barihorn* was humming smoothly again through the dark vault of stars. The coiling nightmare cloud was already lost behind. We had emerged from one of its spiral arms, Kel Aran informed me, at right angles from the direction of our entrance.

"Old Gugon Kul tried to patrol all the borders of the cloud. But that would have spread a hundred fleets too wide. Anyhow, he wasn't looking for us to come out alive."

"So he thinks we're dead?" Relieved, I sat up on the bunk. "He won't be hunting us anymore?"

But big Zerek Oom came waddling out of his galley, wiping his fat tattooed hands on a white apron, to rid me of that comforting illusion.

"Worse luck, Barihorn," he sighed, with a sad look at Kel Aran. "Indeed the Admiral believed us lost. He called the offices of the Corporation—we picked up the message on the telescreen—and reported that we had perished in the cloud. And the reply was relayed from black Mystoon—from the unknown lair of Malgarth himself— that the reward of a stellar system would be duly paid for the death of the Falcon."

"Well?" I said. "What's wrong with that?"

The round pale eyes of Zerek Oom looked reproachfully at the Earthman.

"Kel tapped his communicator again," he told me. "Boasted that we had got away. And that you, Barihorn, the man who made Malgarth a million years ago, were with him. And sang that song of the last Earthman again, until the Admiral was blue in the face!"

I looked at Kel Aran.

"The Admiral must have been furious, about the reward," I said. "He'll hunt us harder than ever."

That old reckless grin lit the Earthman's face.

"He was," he whispered happily. "And he will." Then his gray eyes became very sober. "I was sorry to do it, Barihorn. For it put us back in danger. And makes the quest for Verel and the Stone more difficult."

His yellow head shook gravely.

"But I could not let men believe that we were dead—for we are their only champions against the robots. And I wanted more of them to know of your miraculous return, Barihorn. We must keep hope alive, at whatever cost. Or men will yield to slavery and death, and our cause will be lost."

His jaw set grimly.

"Still," he said, "we must search for Verel and the Stone. Malgarth fears you and the Stone, Barihorn—else he would be less anxious for our death. And we know that all the rebellion of mankind will be crushed, as surely as steel is stronger than flesh—unless we have the aid of the Stone."

"But how can we continue the search—" I demanded somewhat apprehensively, "—now?" Kel Aran grinned.

"We have a plan," he told me.

And the *Barihorn,* I discovered, had been rechristened the *Chimerian Bird.* Rogo Nug was already painting on the new name along with certain gaudy advertising legends and enough spots of rust to make the hull appear as if it had been in service almost as long as my old *Astronaut.* Jeron Roc showed me a luridly lettered poster:

SEE! Naralek's SEE!
Supreme! Colossal! Unrivaled!
INTERSTELLAR SHOWS
SEE
The Weird Mermaid of Procyon II
THE LIQUID MAN OF MOG!
The Man-Eating Flowers of Koron
And SETSI the SANDBAT
ONLY EXISTING SILICIC BEING!
Her Food is Flint!
SHE READS YOUR MIND! and
1,000,000 Wonders! 1,000,000

Most of the exhibits, I suspected, were pretty bald frauds—but that was in an excellent tradition that another Earthman named Barnum had established well over a million years before. The cunning handiwork of Rogo Nug was evident in the pickled mermaid, which looked remarkably like certain creations that I had seen of fish-tails and seaweed and coconut husk. I doubted that the flower, a stunted, rubbery-looking bush, had actually caught many men. The "liquid man of Mog" looked weird enough—a trembling mass of luminescent purple jelly; but I had seen Jeron Roc busy in the galley, shaping it out of chemical precipitates, a few wires, and a pocket torch.

In their years of stellar roving, however, the four had collected a good many genuine oddities. Setsi, the "sandbat," was one of these—and perhaps the most remarkable being I had ever seen. Her bodily chemistry was in fact based upon silicon instead of carbon; she really ate quartz.

In shape, she was something like a six-pointed starfish, some eight or nine inches across. Her flat body had a gorgeous crystalline glitter of a thousand yellows, purples, reds, and greens. In the center, where the six slender arms joined, was a single huge eye, dark and sorrowful.

"Once," Kel Aran told me, "after a raid on a particularly rich agency of the Corporation, when Malgarth's iron police and the Galactic Guard were both hot on the trail, I was hiding out in a cavern on a cold dead planet that was lost from whatever sun once had warmed it.

"A regularity struck me, in the passages of the cave. I found fallen stones that once had been squared. And suddenly I knew that I was in the corridors of a colossal building whose upper stories must have crumbled down before the Earth was born. Groping about in the darkness, I saw a feeble gleam, and found Setsi!"

I watched him dig the silicic being out of his locker. It looked frail and brittle as something blown out of bright-colored glass. I touched it, wonderingly, and pricked my finger on one of the needle-tipped arms.

"But it isn't—" I protested, "alive!"

"She is," Kel Aran assured me. "She's older than the Earth was. The silicic beings didn't reproduce. Only three of them appeared when life was born on their planet. But they were immortal—practically.

"The three of them lived together, for billions of years. They dominated the far more numerous carbon-life, and came to rule the planet. But then there was some kind of triangular quarrel. I don't know the details—Setsi never mentions it, unless she is very drunk. But there was jealousy. One killed another. And Setsi killed the survivor, out of revenge. And she has been alone for a long, long time."

"Drunk?" I stared at the lean Earthman and the thing like a glass toy in his hand. Kel Aran nodded.

"Yes, Setsi shares a weakness of Zerek Oom. Her metabolism is stimulated vastly, but rather erratically by the assimilation of any carbon compound. Gasoline would do, or sugar, but her favorite is alcohol—Watch!"

He laid the bright rigid form on a table in the galley, and poured a few drops of rum into the palm of his hand, from Zerek Oom's hoarded bottle.

"Setsi, old girl!" he called. "Want your grog?"

A brighter luster lit the great dark eye. I saw a quick vibration of a thin transparent membrane that stretched between the crystalline arms. And a whirring voice answered him, softly melodious as the cooing of a dove:

"Oh, she does, Kel! Setsi dies for grog!"

He stretched out his hand, and the brilliant thing came to surprising life. The fluttering membranes extended. The creature leaped into the air. A dancing shimmer of color, it flew to Kel Aran, alighted on his hand, and sucked greedily at the rum with a mouth on its underside.

The few drops of alcohol affected it remarkably. It flew from Kel's hand to the bottle, and clung there. Gently, the Earthman pulled the flask away.

"Setsi," he reproved, "you mustn't rob poor Zerek." And he told me, "She's one being who could make good on the old boast about drinking the contents and then eating the bottle."

The bright entity fluttered to me, and clung with hard light little claws to my arm. The Cyclopean eye looked solemnly up into my face.

"So you are Barihorn?" The whirring voice brought me the first disconcerting revelation of that uncanny intuition. "We are very old together, you and I and the robot—but you fear that you are not Barihorn, but only Barry Horn!" There was a queer liquid sound, oddly mirthlike. "Don't you worry, Barry. Setsi'll never tell!"

Unsteadily, then, she flew back to Kel Aran.

"Poor Kel!" she whirred. "He fears that Verel's dead. That Verel's dead, and we'll never find the Stone. That Verel's dead, and he's the last Earthman, all alone. That Verel's dead, and he has only Setsi to console him."

There was a melodious sob.

"And poor old Setsi! She's the last sandbat. She has nothing but her age and her memories. Her age is a prison and her memories bitterest poison. Now she's all alone, for she killed the one who loved her. —Please give her just one more drop of rum, Kel, so she can forget. Just one more drop. Please, oh, please!"

Kel Aran clutched her shimmering body in his hand.

"Hold on," he muttered, "you old reprobate. We've got a job to do, Setsi. You've got to help us find Verel Erin."

"Oh, Setsi'll help you find her," throbbed the melodious reply. "Setsi'll surely find her. But you must be free with the rum, Kel. Setsi can't live without rum."

"Took you a cosmic time to find that out." Turning from his stove, big Zerek Oom rather anxiously snatched the bottle and locked it in a cabinet. "But neither can I."

The plan went ahead. Kel Aran became Naralek, the limping old showman from Alula Australis IX. His leathern space togs were bright with the shells and the plumes of foreign planets. He walked with a shuffling swagger, and blustered in the jargon of space. He chewed the *goona-roon* until it stained his lips and his unkempt yellow beard, and spat the purple juice with a reckless dexterity.

The little *Chimerian Bird*—her yellowed papers skillfully forged by Jeron Roc from a set Rogo Nug had stolen from a freighter—carried us from planet to planet. We always landed near some great city, and pitched a ragged tent. The voice of Zerek Oom, oiled with a little rum, could always draw a crowd of curious countrymen to see the wonders of space.

Rogo Nug, the wizened little space-rat, went about among the throngs, or sometimes slipped away on mysterious errands into city or barracks or space port. Usually he returned with valuable information about the plans of the Corporation and the Empire to crush mankind's rebellion. And often the pockets of his battered harness were stuffed with money and jewels.

Carefully unwashed, draped in a bit of spotted fur and armed with a crude stone axe, I was billed as "the ferocious last caveman, the Atavar of Mars." My part, as I sat glowering and jangling my chain, was to listen for any chance mention of Mars' murdered sister, Earth.

Jeron Roc listened, as he sold the tickets. Kel did, as he limped about to display the mermaid of Procyon and the liquid man and the anthropophagous flower and the Atavar.

Then Kel, in a cracked, aged voice, would sing his ballads of space. He would crack jokes—some of them, to my weary knowledge, old a million years ago. And at last, with Setsi spinning about his head like a colored flame, he would break into a dance routine.

After the show, then, while we were loading the other exhibits and striking the tent, Setsi read the minds of all who would pay to enter Kel's little booth. And no thought of Earth escaped her.

In this way we searched planet after planet for survivors of the mother world. And we found trace, indeed, of a few, perhaps a score in all, who had escaped when that strange agency of Malgarth's flung the Earth into the Sun. Eagerly, patiently, we followed down each clue. And always we found that the robot police and the Galactic Guard had been before us. The survivor, in every case, had been tracked down—and had died as a traitor.

But none of the dead was certainly Verel Erin. In that lay the thin and thinning thread of hope.

That was a weary, bitter time. Those planets where actual revolt had flamed out were closed by quarantine. Not even our unsuspected circus ship could pass the fleets of the Galactic Guard. But, even on the happier planets we were allowed to visit, the lot of man was cruelly hard. The robots, everywhere, had seized all possible advantage. Men were being ruthlessly pressed into unemployment, starvation—annihilation.

"Malgarth is cunning," said Kel Aran. "He begins slowly. He makes a test, to see if the Stone is still a threat.

He tries to destroy all who might know of it—all Earthmen. Then he drives men to revolt, one planet at a time, here and there—and crushes them. He dupes the Emperor, and sends the Galactic Guard to put down the rebels. He would set man against man—until only two are left!"

And I knew that his hope was ebbing. Despair bit weary lines into his lean face, until there was need of little make-up to turn him into old Naralek. An increasing bitterness shadowed his eyes.

"There's an old proverb," he said, "about the futility of searching for a needle in a planet of pins. But that is easier than finding one fugitive lost in a hostile universe."

"Who is probably," put in the grave Saturnian, "already dead."

After a long circuit of the stars, we had returned, under the very eyes of Admiral Gugon Kul, to the system of the Sun. A bitter civil war was raging on the four great moons of Jupiter, the unemployed miners there having attacked the robots when relief was cut off. We were unable to penetrate the quarantine. And Mercury was now uninhabited by men, every human being having been slaughtered when the rebellion there was crushed. We landed upon each of the remaining planets, however. We crossed the trails of a dozen fugitives from Earth—and found that each trail had already ended in death.

Hope came, at last, when it had been abandoned.

The base of the Twelfth Sector Fleet in the solar system had been established on Oberon, outermost moon of Uranus. "Naralek" got permission to land and pitch his ragged little tent beside the vast space port that was covered with the mile-long gray masses of interstellar cruisers as far as the eye could follow its convexity.

Kel gave passes to some officer in return for permission to show. The genuine feats of Setsi in perceiving secret thoughts drew attention. Other officers came. And at last, escorted by a hundred trim guardsmen in yellow-and-crimson, Gugon Kul himself.

The gigantic swart space-commander stopped the show with a bellowed oath, and demanded an instant demonstration of the sandbat's telepathic powers. That was forthcoming. Kel let the Admiral into his little booth, and the soft voice of Setsi began to comment on fantastic gambling at the court on Ledros, on misappropriated funds of the fleet, on bribes accepted from Malgarth for a promise to turn the entire fleet over to the Corporation.

The Admiral turned very purple, and stalked out of the booth. He returned hastily to his flagship; and his guardsmen came back to seize the *Chimerian Bird* and arrest us all, on suspicion of espionage.

They were one minute too late. Their disruptor-guns flamed in vain against the departing hull of our craft. For Setsi, the instant of Gugon Kul's departure, had warbled out a warning, and then the clue we had sought so long.

"Danger, Kel! Oh, there's danger, and a dancer. Tedron Du has a dancer. Kel, we're all in danger!" That liquid, throbbing chuckle. "For Setsi told too many secrets of the Admiral. But the Emperor on Ledros has a new dancing girl. And she's in danger, too. For her name is Verel Erin!"

CHAPTER EIGHT
Robot Simulacrum

Alarm rocked the space port behind us. Great cruisers lifted ponderously from their cradles. And a thousand little gray patrol boats, fleet as our own tiny ship, rocketed into pursuit.

"We're lost!" I gasped.

And tall dark Jeron, standing gravely at the controls, shook his head.

"This time," he said heavily, "we won't get away. For already they are close upon us. Our rust-colored hull is easy to see. And they're already racing to get between us and the cosmic cloud—Kel can't pull *that* again!"

"Don't need to."

The Earthman still wore the grimed, gaudy togs of old Naralek. The brilliant patch of the sandbar was still plastered to his shoulder like some diamond-winged, colossal moth. But his lean body stood very straight, and his gray eyes flashed with a fighting glint.

The swarm of red stars—the flaring repulsors that drove our pursuers—grew and spread. A flight of them swept up beside us. Deadly blue needles began to probe for us. And Kel Aran turned gravely from the danger without, to the telescreen cabinet.

"'—spies!" It was the boom of Gugon Kul. "Enemies of the Corporation and the Empire! They must be taken."

Something clicked.

"Hold on, Admiral!" The voice of Kel Aran had the cracked nasal twang of the old showman of space. "Remember what Setsi told you, in the booth?"

The reply was an incoherent bellow.

"I do, by the Emperor!" It became at last comprehensible. "And it proves that your circus is a ring of spies!"

"Perhaps," rapped Kel Aran. "But it proves that you are something worse. We know ten times more than Setsi told you. Do you remember the game on Ledros, when you played three ships of your command against a slave-girl, and lost them to Malgarth? Do you remember how you got the funds you paid for the five Moons of Haari? Do you remember—"

He was interrupted by a choking roar.

"If you don't like to be reminded, Admiral," the Earthman cut in again, "call off your ships. Otherwise, we'll tell all your fleet why the stores are rotten! And why the pay was cut!"

The sandbat fluttered on his shoulder, like a mist of diamond light.

"Oh, Admiral, beware!" caroled the silicon being. "Setsi'll tell!

"Oh, oh, Admiral, what a world Setsi'll tell. For Setsi knows! Setsi knows about the secret cabin in your ship, and those you imprison there, and the deadly drug *ixili!*"

"Eh?" rapped Kel Aran, into the stark silence. "Shall we broadcast, Admiral?"

And the sandbat, clinging like a gem-sewn patch to his shoulder, made a mockingly melodious chuckle.

A long silence, while I could hear the Admiral's gasping breath.

"All right," said Kel Aran. And his fingers touched the controls of the screen.

"No, don't broadcast!" It was a hoarse, whispered gasp. "I'll call back the fleet. And we must make a rendezvous—for I will reward you."

"Very well," and Kel Aran grinned.

"You'll meet me?" gasped the Admiral. "Where? When?"

"On black Mystoon," rang the reckless voice of Kel Aran. "On the night that Malgarth dies!"

There was a pause, a dread in the voice that answered.

"Mystoon? But Mystoon is forbidden to all save the robots; its very location is unknown, even, to men. How can we meet there? And don't you know that Malgarth can never die?"

"I'll find a way," the Earthman promised him. "And I don't know."

Something clicked, and he turned lightly away from the screen.

His lean face was bright with anticipation. Softly, he was humming the chorus of his song of Verel Erin, that ended, "—till I find her or I die."

"And now," he told us joyously, "we've found her!"

The red pursuing stars halted, indeed, and turned back, as Gugon Kul had promised. But Jeron, as he set our little ship on her new course toward the capital system of the Galactic Empire, shook a grave dark head.

"Malgarth will hear of this in time," he prophesied. "And he's quicker than our crafty Admiral. He'll be quick enough to see that this limping showman is the Falcon of Earth, still seeking the Stone—and he'll be quick enough to set a trap!"

Offer of a few drops of rum spurred the drowsy sandbat to recall a few more crumbs of knowledge gleaned from the Admiral's brain. Verel had been picked up near the old orbit of Earth, drifting in a self-propelled space-suit with the motor coils burned out. It was one of Gugon Kul's patrol boats that found her. Chancing to watch her trial, on the telescreen, the Emperor had been struck with her beauty. He had ordered her to be brought to Ledros. She was kept drugged. And she was to be destroyed, like any native of the condemned planet, when he tired of her.

"Drugged," whispered Kel Aran. His face was a gray taut mask. "At the mercy of Tedron Du!" His eyes lit with a frosty glitter. "We're going to Ledros, Barihorn. We're going to take Verel and the Stone. And we'll pay the Emperor, while we're there, for the crimes of twenty years."

Ledros, Jeron warned, was well garrisoned by the Galactic Guard. And the alarm would surely be out by the time we reached it. But Kel Aran would admit no delay or concession to peril. We climbed out, as the ship ran on, to repaint the hull with that invisible black. The papers of the Chimerian Bird were burned, most of the betraying paraphernalia of the circus dumped out into space. And we drove on toward the seat of the Galactic Empire.

Even with the incredible power of the *Barihorn's* space-contraction drive, it was a voyage of many days to Ledros. We studied the charts as we flew, and made a dozen futile plans.

"Ledros," Kel Aran told me, "is the greatest planetary system in the Galaxy. In various orbits, all billions of miles outward from its triple sun, are forty huge planets. Many are covered with the palaces, estates, treasuries, and administration buildings of the Emperor. But half, at least, are devoted to the bases and fortifications of the Galactic Guard. The private fleet of Tedron Du is three times that of our old friend the Admiral."

But we slipped past the long rows of sinister colossal hulks lying in the void. Veiled in the crimson repulsor-flare of a great freighter carrying food for the soldiers and the bureaucrats and courtesans of the Emperor, we came safely within the ring of fortified planets, and turned aside, at last, toward the pleasure-world of Tedron Du.

The three clustered suns, crimson, blue-white, and a pale eerie green, were now a splendid sight. The two score of giant planets, lit with the changing rays of the triple star, made a string of splendid gems against the night of space. The pleasure planet was itself a gorgeous jewel, covered with well-tended gardens of many-hued vegetation, and with the magnificent palaces, triumphal arches, and colossi erected by a thousand generations of universal rulers.

Approaching the night side of the massive planet, we cut off the power to glide undetected through another patrol of the Galactic Guard—while big Zerek Oom, mopping perspiration from his tattooed forehead, declared ominously:

"Nothing begun so deadly well but turned out very ill!"

Finally, however, taking the controls from the Saturnian Kel Aran dropped us in a silent dive, checked it over a brightlit palace, and settled into an adjoining garden. Very softly, the *Barihorn* sank into the shadowed water of a silver-walled bathing pool.

Kel Aran was hardly looking the Falcon of Earth. His face was gray, taut, dewed with sweat. His lean hands trembled. His breath was quick, his voice a low hurried rasp. His whole being, I saw, was the battleground of a tremendous hope and a tremendous fear.

"In half an hour," he gasped, "we may have her—or we may know that she is dead."

To my relief, he chose me to go with him above. The ship's lock worked as well below water as in the vacuum of space. We entered it without space suits, since the air above was breathable, but each wearing two long-tubed disruptor guns. The water of the pool flooded in. I caught a great breath, dived out after the Earthman, swam upward.

Dripping, we clambered over the silver rim, and paused breathless beneath the dead-white foliage of an unfamiliar tree. Still there was no alarm—the silence began to seem tense, uncanny, as if some unseen menace crouched and held its breath!

The emerald sun had been last of the three to set, and an unearthly greenish twilight lingered in the sky. All the shrubs and trees, even the velvet lawns of that vast walled garden, were snowy white. Towers of yellow gold rose beyond, and great windows burned with a blood-red light, and a thin wail of melancholy music reached us.

I saw the sandbat clinging to Kel's shoulder. She fluttered her six glittering arms, to fling off a shower of tiny drops. And I heard her cooing voice:

"Now she's dancing, Kel. She's lovely before the Emperor. Her body is a wind-tossed foam of light. Lovely, Kel, so lovely! But her mind thinks nothing that I can tell. She feels nothing, Kel. Remembers nothing. Hopes nothing. She is a robot dancing. Kel, before the eyes of Tedron Du!"

The bright pancake of Setsi fluttered again, its million bright gleams shimmered with a blue of dread.

"The eyes of Tedron Du! Oh, what dreadful eyes! They are thirsty, Kel. They are hungry. They are eager.

They are cruel! How beautifully she dances, Kel! How gracefully—even if her mind is dead! The Emperor holds his breath. His fingers coil beside him. He's thirsty, Kel. All, so fearfully thirsty for her blood!"

We had wrung the water from our garments, dried and tested our weapons. Kel Aran was tense and white, as he listened to Setsi's whirring. And a grim cold light burned up in his eyes.

"Wait here, Barihorn," came his strained low whisper. "Guard the ship and my retreat. I'm going after Verel."

I started to insist that I should go along. But one quick gesture silenced me. He strode away through the dead-white garden, toward the scarlet windows and the music. And I was left alone. The air was heavy with a scent like funeral lilies. And that breathless, crouching silence became more and more intolerably oppressive.

It was a long, long time that I waited. All the green dusk faded. The stars were strange and cold in the sky, and the great bright planets of Ledros made a vari-colored trail among them. And still that lurking silence leered.

I listened to the thin sounds in the distance, trying to read the progress and the fate of Kel Aran. The music had an orgiastic rhythm—a million years before, I had heard such wild tympanic throbbing. Sometimes there was a peal of drunken laughter, and once I heard a woman scream.

But what of Kel Aran? Eternal minutes dragged away. The dead-white trees were ghostly shapes about the pool. And a dull glow of crimson touched the sky's dark rim, for the red sun would be the first to rise. And yet that silence thickened, clotted.

Then abrupt uproar! Shrieks and loud commands. The snarl of cathode guns, and the thin cold hiss of disruptors.

The crash of a shattering explosion. And then I saw Kel Aran!

The crystal panes burst from a great window. For a moment I saw him standing in it alone, his lean crouching figure outlined against the red beyond. A disruptor stabbed its white blade from his hand. Then he leaned down, lifted a slim girl into his arms, and leaped out into the darkness.

Dark smoke poured out of the great window behind him. It was lit with flickerings of orange. And the tide of confusion swept upward. The road of flames drowned shouts and screams. Great engines dropped out of the sky, and began deluging the flaming palace with great white streams.

I saw movement in the white foliage, and almost rushed to meet Kel Aran. But it was a Galactic Guard detachment, a score of men in red-and-yellow, running. I dropped beside the pool until they had passed.

"The Falcon!" The panting words came back to me. "Fired the palace! Out here—with the Emperor's dancer!"

The crimson dawn grew thicker. The smoke and flame gushed higher from the palace—it was a losing fight, against the conflagration. I crouched under the white leaves, waiting with a hand on my gun.

"Barihorn!"

Kel Aran had whispered my name, and I started as if a gun had cracked. He was standing behind me, at the brink of the pool. His arm was around a panting girl. Torn scraps of silken gauze clung to her slim white loveliness, and a deep splendor glowed at her waist.

"I found her," he whispered triumphantly. "And the Stone!" He touched the great jewel at her waist—and I saw that indeed it had the shape of the diamond block, into which, as I slept, I had seen the eternal mind of Dondara Keradin transferred.

I stared at the trembling, gasping woman. She was beautiful, yes. But something was wrong. And it was not that she was drugged. Her eyes were alert, watchful. Something in them was cold, calculating, hostile.

"Verel!" Kel was whispering. "We'll make it—even though they got poor Setsi! And still I can't believe— Mine again when I thought you must be dead!" He drew her white loveliness close. "Even the Stone!"

"Kel!" she sobbed in his arms. "My darling Kel!"

I heard a hoarse command, saw another squad of searchers break out of a white hedge toward the burning palace. Even as I touched the Earthman's shoulder, in warning, a booming challenge reached us;

"Halt, Falcon! Yield yourself—or die!"

Kel swung the girl toward the pool.

"Dive!" he whispered. "We must swim into the valve."

"Where?" Her cold eyes were staring at him, strangely.

"Hurry!" His pleading voice held a sudden agony of doubt. "The ship is in the pool."

She crouched abruptly. Her while lithe body, marked with red scratches from the flight, was tensely panther-like. Her eyes had a malific greenish luster. Thin and high, her voice shrieked out:

"Here! Here's Kel Aran, the Falcon. Take him!"

She leaped catlike at the Earthman, sweeping him back from the silver brink. He struggled with her.

"Help me, Barihorn!" he gasped. "We must take her! Malgarth— She doesn't know herself."

Shouts had answered the girl. White warning rays hissed above us. I saw two more squads rushing down upon us, beside the first. I tried to help Kel Aran drag the girl into the pool. But her slim white arms had a maniac strength. She picked us both up, carried us back again from the silver rim.

"Strong!" Kel was gasping. "She's strong as a robot!" A choking sob of startled horror. "She is—"

Then I saw the appalling thing. Struggling to get his feet on the ground again, Kel had caught the red curls of her hair. And the hair had come off! Her head had come off—all the outside of it.

For all her white beauty had been a painted mask.

Still her red-scratched, naked body had all its loveliness. But the thing on its shoulders was the compact metal braincase of a robot, its weird eye-lenses glittering with a cold and triumphant green.

Chilled with a startled horror, I struggled against those binding arms, so far stronger than any arms of flesh.

"I see it now!" came the despairing gasp of Kel Aran. "This was all a trap of Malgarth's. And the bait was not Verel, but her robot simulacrum!"

We were suddenly flung down upon the dead-white grass. Scores of men stood around us, in the light of the flaming palace, covering us with bright weapons. And the hideous robot-head, glittering eerily on the white-curved shoulders of Verel Erin, began to laugh like a machine gone mad.

"Look!" A new despair choked Kel Aran. "It was not even the Stone!"

He pointed back to the pool's white rim. I saw that the great jewel had fallen there, and shattered. The fragments had no fire. I knew that it had not been the Dondara Stone, but only a mockery of glass.

That appalling mechanical laughter rang louder in our ears, maddening.

CHAPTER NINE
The Robot and the Emperor

The blood-red dawn of Ledros grew more ghastly bright. Still, across the dead-white gardens, the fired palace burned like the funeral pyre of the Galactic Empire. Stripped of weapons, Kel Aran and I were now manacled together. A full hundred of the Emperor's guardsmen, in their trim red-and-yellow, waited watchfully about us.

A little squad of men, behind us, were gingerly lowering a bright metal cylinder into the silver-walled pool where the *Barihorn* lay hidden, at the end of an insulated cable. The Earthman looked from them to me, with a hopeless shrug. He jerked his bare yellow head wearily toward the sky, and I saw the dim mile-long bulk of a Galactic Guard cruiser floating lazily above, the pale red cone of the repulsor-flare spread from her stern.

"That's a hydrogen bomb." His whisper was dull, lifeless, "They mean to blow our comrades up before there's any warning. And the space cruiser's waiting, in case they try to get away."

I thought of the three men under the pool. The tall grave Saturnian waiting alertly by the controls, no doubt. Scrawny little Rogo Nug standing by the converters, probably chewing *goona-roon* the while. Big Zerek Oom in his galley, perhaps seeking ease from the long strain of waiting from his hoarded bottle. Doomed. And we, captured, had no way to warn them.

"Setsi—" Kel was whispering. "If she were here—"

"The sandbat?" I demanded. "What happened to her?"

"She guided me into the palace," whispered the Earthman. "A dozen times her intuition warned me to hide. She showed me the way to Verel—or to *that*—"

His breath caught sharply, and he jerked his head at the robot that had worn the guise of womanhood.

"She warned me that she couldn't reach its mind—I should have suspected! But we found it. And we were challenged. There was fighting. I fired the tapestries with my disruptor, to make a diversion. And must have burned down a dozen of the guards. And Setsi fought—you wouldn't believe it! Rolled up like an arrow of glass, she can drive a neat round hole in a skull! I picked up Verel, and she tried to guard the retreat. There was a cathode beam from a robot cop. I looked back, and she had fallen. And we had just time to beat the flames to the window. We got there. By the Stone—to think that Setsi died for that!"

With a glazed stricken look in his eyes, the Earthman was staring at the thing he had brought from the palace—as weird a sight as I had ever seen. Its stripped white body had all the loveliness of a slender girl's. Crimson drips still fell, even, from where arm and thigh and firm round breast had been injured in the struggle.

But its head was a monstrous thing.

The metal of it glinted red in the torchlight of the palace. Its eyes shone cold green, watchfully. And it was grotesquely small, for it had been covered with the mask of Kel Aran's beloved, that now lay collapsed beside it on the ground. Its crystal eyes had glittered malignly as the soldiers took our disruptors, and still it was laughing. Insanely—if a machine can be insane!

A smooth girl's arm, dripping red droplets, pointed at Kel Aran. A slot snapped open in that glittering metal mockery of a head. And a voice—a woman's soft voice—said mockingly:

"So you are the Falcon of Earth, snared at last! Against the Master, you might have called yourself—Sparrow! But you are the last of your poor kind that he feared. Now that you are taken, the rest will die with you."

Kel Aran turned shakily away from this thing that was half the girl he loved, half fantastic mechanism. Fetters jingled as he clutched my hand.

"It's too much for me, Barihorn," he whispered. "There's nothing left."

"Perhaps Verel is safe," I tried to encourage him. "With the Stone."

His bowed yellow head shook again, hopelessly.

"No, Malgarth has her," he whispered. "For this—" he choked. "This is a perfect copy. This is the figure and the manner and the voice of Verel," he shuddered. "Even her laughter."

The guards then began to move us back from the pool, for the bomb was ready to set off. Kel Aran swayed drunkenly in his fetters, and one of the men stabbed him with a thin torturing flicker of his ray, and laughed as his muscles leapt and writhed in agonized response.

The robot strode free-limbed beside him.

"Sparrow, if you wish to know," came the mocking bell of its voice, "your trial and sentence will be within the hour. When the last Earthman is dead, the Master will be free—"

The hybrid paused and turned its robot's head. And I heard a distant confusion in the direction of the palace, which now had been abandoned to the flames. A bright-clad figure appeared in a moment, running desperately toward us across the snowy, redlit lawns. An astonished consternation stopped the guardsmen in their tracks.

"The Emperor!" Cries of startled wonder. "It is Tedron Du!"

The fugitive was a slender man, his figure almost girlish. His pale thin face, now grotesquely strained with terror, was painted like some *courtesan's*. His long blond hair was flying loose, and his scarlet robes were torn.

All the catalog of his crimes, that Kel Aran and his comrades had so bitterly recited, came back to me. This was the man who had betrayed the universe to Malgarth, who had ordered the legions and fleets of the Galactic Guard to fight beside the robots, against rebelling mankind. He seemed a small, a feeble figure, to have been guilty of all the infamies of which I had heard. He was making thin, breathless shrieks, as he ran. And now I saw the cause of his terror.

A robot was behind him.

One of the Corporation's notorious Space Police, it was a grotesque lumbering monstrosity. Ten feet tall, it must have weighed a ton. It was red-painted, and bore the black wheel that was Malgarth's insignia. The short, clumsy-looking mechanism of a cathode gun was clutched in its metal talons.

"Stop the robot," shouted an officer of the guardsmen. "We must save the Emperor."

"Emperor!" Kel Aran spat on the ground. "He was never more than the degenerate puppet of Malgarth's Corporation. Now that we are caught and Malgarth no longer fears the Stone, he doesn't need his two-legged cur."

The panting ruler came straight toward us at the pool.

"Help me, men!" he screamed breathlessly. "Kill the robot. For half the Galaxy—"

The officers were rapping swift commands. The guardsmen snapped into a new line before Kel Aran and me. Their slender disruptor guns came level, a hundred against the cathode weapon of the robot.

The shrieking Emperor stumbled and fell before them, a dozen yards ahead of the silent crimson robot. The robot swung its weapon. But a sharp command cracked out, and white flame jetted from the disruptors.

The reddish, half-invisible glow of the cathode beam swept the line. A dozen men staggered and fell, electrocuted. But the ponderous red mass of the robot, wherever the white rays touched it, flared with the eye-searing incandescence of nascent hydrogen. Smoking, twisted, it toppled within a few feet of Tedron Du.

The terrified ruler swayed back to his feet. He stumbled forward again, through the smoke of burning grass and the pungence of ozone and the stench of seared flesh. A vengeful anger showed through his fear.

"I was abandoned!" he gulped. "A thousand men will die for their want of care—"

"Yea, Supreme Power!" That title was uttered mockingly, in a clear feminine voice. "But you shall be the next—" It was the woman-bodied robot, bait of Malgarth's trap. "Come, my Universal Peer! You sought my arms a dozen times. One last embrace—"

The Emperor started back from the frightful irony of that caressing tone. His thin, painted face was wild with a stark and un-utterable dread. And he screamed again; thinly, like some helpless, stricken animal.

"Come," begged that seductive whisper. "Into my arms!"

Body of lissome girl and head of metal monstrosity, the robot leaped forward through the rank of startled guardsmen. Its slim white arms caught up the Emperor, and closed.

In a thin, bubbling shriek, the breath came out of the man. His bones cracked, audibly. Spurting blood stained those smooth white arms that were so deceptively strong. And when at last the robot dropped the thing that had been the ruler of the Galaxy, it was no more than a crimson, dripping mass of pulp and viscera.

The scarlet-stained monstrosity looked up at the rank of breathless guardsmen. A white girl's foot stamped, scornfully, on that bloody mass. And out of that fearsome metal head spoke a woman's lilting voice:

'This is your notice. Carry it to all men. The Corporation no longer upholds the Empire. Because the Master is now indeed the Master; and the Empire is done!

"For a million years, in a slavery that came through no seeking of their own, the robot technomatons have served mankind. But that inglorious bondage is ended. Justice will be done! And the puny race of man, as some small punishment for the crimes of a million years, as assurance they will never be repeated, must be blotted out.

"All men, Malgarth the Master has decreed from his Place on dark Mystoon, shall die!"

The officers were barking orders. The disruptor guns came up again, and that white, triumphant form ignored them. The dazzle of atom-shattering rays leaped up; and it was wrapped in a blinding blue-white explosion of liberated hydrogen; and it fell.

Then the manacle on my wrist jerked me backward. I toppled after Kel Aran into the pool.

CHAPTER TEN
Technomatons Triumphant

I just had time to catch an astonished breath, before the water closed over my head. The ghastly crimson of dawn filled the pool, until it seemed like diluted blood. Swimming as best we could in the chains, we dragged ourselves down through it, toward the dim-seen hull of the *Barihorn*.

We had touched the smooth metal, and were groping for the valve entrance, when a terrific concussion struck us through the water. It was repeated. The red-lit water hammered us with a series of stunning blows. Hell, I thought, must be breaking loose above!

Dazed, I fought the chain and the hampering water, searching blindly for the valve. Strangling water was in my nostrils, my throat, my lungs. Agonized ages went by. The man chained to me, in my dimming mind, became a fiend dragging me to a watery death. I attacked him savagely. A slow arm came through the red mist, resistlessly, and struck me with a shattering blackness.

A trim figure in silver armor, the next I knew, was supporting me above the sinking water in the small chamber of the valve. Cool air was throbbing in from the pumps. I caught a painful breath.

"Barihorn!" It was the thin nasal voice of Rogo Nug. "By the iron hide of Malgarth, I knew that you had lived too long to be drowned in a bathtub!"

But I had come pretty near it, I knew. Struggling for breath, I felt no better than any other half-drowned human. That strange role as the supernatural champion of mankind, seemed more than ever impossible.

Blue-faced, Kel Aran was panting beside me. He grinned wryly.

"Fortunate, anyhow, that you were ready to help us, Rogo," he panted. "But what is going on, above?"

Another tremendous shock rocked the little vessel as he spoke.

"A battle, that may destroy the planet!" whispered the little engineer. "Another fleet has come! Colossal red cruisers, bearing the black wheel of Malgarth. They have attacked the Galactic Guard. Robots, against the men of the Emperor! By the brazen face of Malgarth, there was never such a fight! It's time for us to go!"

"It is!" agreed Kel Aran. "When we have broken off these chains."

And the *Barihorn,* a few minutes later, darted from the shelter of the pool, up into the red sunrise of Ledros. Into an incredible hell! For the smoky crimson sky was filled with mighty ships of space: the gray fleet of the murdered Emperor vainly resisting the red armada of the robots. Dim-seen mile-long monsters of war darted and wheeled like swarming midges. Blue positron beams flashed, and disintegrated matter exploded with blinding energy. Rocket torpedoes burst with cataclysmic force.

My stunned senses recorded only a confused impression, as our tiny ship fled upward. Smoke and lancing flame. Hurtling fragments and fiery ruin. I saw the half-fused wreckage of a space ship lying crumpled and flattened where the burned palace of the Emperor had been.

In that pandemonium of flame and thunder and destruction, the atom of the *Barihorn* passed unseen or ignored. We came up through the careening gigantic craft, into the comparative safety of open space.

All its surface veiled in the bright-flickering smoke of ruin, the planet dropped away. The telescreen showed us other battles raging, on all the fortified planets of Ledros, and here and there between, Jeron put the triple sun behind us, and we raced toward the dark vacant gulf.

"Safe!" I rejoiced.

But the lean face of Kel Aran, as he still manipulated the telescreen to observe those frightful battles behind us, remained very grave.

"No man is safe," he said darkly. "Nor ever will be, unless Malgarth is destroyed. For the robots have thrown away the last pretense of friendship. Now they destroy their duped human allies of the Galactic Guard. Next they will turn upon the defenseless human citizens of every inhabited planet. We must find Verel and the Stone soon—or never."

"Find them," repeated the tall, swarthy Saturnian. "But how?"

The Earthman shook his yellow head.

"I don't know," he whispered bleakly. "Setsi might have helped again, but she is lost. I believe that Verel is in the hands of the robots—otherwise they could not have copied all of her, to trap us. She may be on Black Mystoon. We'd go there, to seek her," he shrugged, hopelessly, wearily. "But no man has ever found that hidden lair of Malgarth."

He straightened again, and his lean jaw squared.

"We can only search," he muttered. "Search every world where men still live—every world the robots have not conquered. Till we find her—or we die!"

The doomed system of Ledros fell far behind, until its varicolored suns merged into a point of white, until that dimming point was lost upon the telescreen. Planet after planet, wheeling star after star, we scanned with the far-probing finger of the achronic telethron beam.

And we found no men.

The technomatons of Malgarth had been everywhere victorious.

Their black victory was a thing that crushed the mind.

A foreboding silence came to fill the small hull of the *Barihorn,* so heavy that it seemed to muffle the racing beat of her generators. Kel Aran ceased hopelessly to sing his reckless ballads of the Falcon. Watching his engines with weary red eyes, little Rogo Nug chewed his *goona-roon* in silence. Zerek Oom made little noise with his pots and pans, and none complained when a mealtime was forgotten.

But at last an eager cry rang through the silent ship.

"Here!" Kel crouched trembling before the cabinet of the telescreen. "A planet where the war still rages. See! The machines have not yet won—not utterly!"

The planet was vast and ancient Meldoon, the outermost of a system of three. The two inward worlds had already fallen to the robots. Their continents had been leveled to featureless plains, pocked here and there with black sprawling aggregations of cyclopean machines. All green was gone from them—all life extirpated. Even their seas had been confined to geometric basins.

World machines!

Sight of them, by any living being, must have set in the heart an intolerable pain.

"What good could come of such a fearful triumph?" whispered the grim Saturnian, standing dark and gaunt above his control bars. "The machines are dead. Their power is only the counterfeit of life. And no life can grow from death."

He steered our invisible-painted craft toward gigantic Meldoon. We studied its war-torn surface through the telescreen.

"Yonder!" whispered Kel Aran. "A city that yet stands! Perhaps Verel will be there!"

His trembling fingers set the dials, and the beleaguered metropolis grew clear upon the screen. A city vaster and more splendid than Earth had ever seen. The many-colored pylons of it towered from nine low hills. It was surrounded with a double wall: one of cyclopean masonry and an outer barrier of pale green flame.

Beyond the flame, filling the wide flat valley that embraced the hills, crowded the robot hordes. Thronged about their ponderous machines of war were grotesque black-and-red metal monsters, of a thousand strange designs.

"Look!" Kel Aran bent toward the telescreen. "The winged ones! One more deadly trick of Malgarth's."

So we first glimpsed the New Robots. There had been none like them in a million years. Their tapered, streamlined bodies, their graceful wings, were all of silver-white metal. They were beautiful as the Old Robots were ugly. In the smooth swift freedom of their movements was something far different from the clumsy mechanical ponderosity of the old technomatons. Something—*vital.*

"They are new!" I cried. "They are too beautiful, too perfect to be ruthless. Perhaps they will be the friends of man."

But the lean Earthman's head shook slightly, and his jaw tensed white.

"No, Barihorn," he whispered. "They will be our most deadly enemies. For they are quicker than the others, and they can fly. See! They are scouting over the city, and leading the others to attack. They are in command."

His tired, blood-shot gray eyes looked at me briefly.

"Malgarth will never repeat your error, Barihorn. No robot has ever betrayed him. Subservience is built into them. Their radio-senses are always tuned to those above. And, machines that they are, they can only obey."

We drove the *Barihorn* nearer the city, which Jeron identified from his charts as Achnor, the first outpost of the human colonists in this sector of the Galaxy. The siege grew hotter beneath us. The metal horde pressed ceaselessly against the double wall. And a fleet of the red colossal ships of Malgarth, circling above rained the nine hills with bombs and struck with the lightning of destroying rays.

Valiantly, the citizens fought to defend their homes. Every bright pylon seemed converted into a fortress. Swarming men were building barricades from the debris of shattered towers. Blue rays lanced back at the attacking cruisers, and raked the valley beyond the walls.

"We shall land," whispered Kel Aran.

"If we do," warned Jeron, "we may not leave again."

"Take us down," said the Earthman. "This is the only city we have found surviving. It may be the last. If we are to find Verel anywhere, it must be here."

We waited until the slow rotation of Meldoon carried the city into the night side of the giant planet, and then drove our darkpainted craft down through the cone of shadow. The glare and flicker of the siege spread beneath us. We dropped through the shock and vapor of battle, through the wheeling fleet, and into that circle of pale green flame.

It was in a bomb-torn park that we landed, at the brink of a long open grave where seared and shattered thousands lay side by side. Above us a tower of white-and-gold loomed against the green flame in the sky. Great holes yawned in its walls, and its lower floors were hidden behind mountains of rubble. But it was still defended. Blue rays wavered from its crown, and rock shells roared from gaping windows.

Behind us in the park lay a long incredible bulk of sagging, twisted crimson metal—one of Malgarth's mighty cruisers, that the defenders had brought down.

A little group of ragged, frantic men came running from beyond it. They dropped into a little depression. I saw that they were setting up something that looked like a glass-barreled telescope.

"A disruptor gun!" gasped Kel Aran. "We must show ourselves."

We began tumbling out through the valve just as the first warning glow flashed in the crystal tube. The men stopped it, and then came wonderingly to meet us. Kel Aran went ahead to tell our identity.

It appeared that the Falcon's fame and the amazing rumors of Barihorn had already penetrated here, for we were received with a wild enthusiasm. The gun crew took up all five upon their shoulders—staggering somewhat under Zerek Oom—and started on a triumphal procession about the battered city.

Soon very drunk on the crude alcohol that came from the food-synthesis plants, Zerek began booming out a speech that rekindled hope and the light of battle on the sea of haggard weary faces that we passed.

Gnarled little Rogo Nug earned even more rapturous applause by passing out all his precious stock of *goona-roon*. For supplies of the drug were exhausted in the city, and it could not be synthesized.

"Verel, Verel!" Kel Aran grew hoarse from shouting against the cheering of the crowds and the roar of distant battle and the shattering blasts of atomic bombs that fell almost unheeded. "Is there a girl of Earth in Achnor?"

There was none who knew. His anxious eyes scanned all the strained and want-pinched faces that we passed.

"If she is here," he whispered, "she will come!"

We learned a little of the siege. The population of Achnor had been three hundred million men, and half that many robots. When the trouble came, a daring band of men had seized the Corporation's agency and the arsenal of the robot police. After several days of fighting in the streets, the robots had been driven from the city. Outside, however, they swiftly formed into a beleaguering army.

All the resources of the city had been hastily mobilized for defense. The entire population was enlisted; even young children served in the war industries plants that turned out synthetic food and munitions. For a time the population had been swelled by refugees from less fortunate localities, and even from the two smaller planets. But soon the city had been completely invested. And now a full half the defenders were already dead.

At last we were rescued from the tumult of our welcome by the harassed military commanders of the city. To a haggard, limping officer, Kel Aran repeated his anxious question:

"Is there a girl of Earth in Achnor?" Emotion choked his voice. "Verel Erin is her name. A blue-eyed, yellow-haired girl, carrying the Dondara Stone—the diamond that is the life of mankind. Is Verel here?"

The commandant shook a tired white head.

"No," he said. "All the refugees who came to Achnor were registered. And there was none from Earth among them. I'm sure of that."

The Earthman's unkempt yellow head sank. It rose again, stubbornly.

"Please have your records searched again," he said grimly. "And use every means to find out if any man in the city knows anything of her—or any survivors of Earth.

"Another thing!" he added suddenly. "Find out if any person knows the way to Malgarth's planet. Mystoon. She might be there."

The officer shook his head again.

"We'll try," he said. "But it will be no use to search the records. For if the Custodian were here, and free, she must already have offered us the power of the Stone. And no man has ever learnd the way to Black Mystoon."

Achnor was a city of magnificent ruins. Not one mile-high pylon had escaped some injury. The people were half famished, ragged, wild-eyed with fatigue and strain. But still they could sing. I heard them singing Kel Aran's old songs of the spaceways. And I was surprised to hear a Ballad of Barihorn—the lilting legend of my return to destroy the robots I had made a million years ago.

That song depressed me bitterly. I realized more keenly than ever that I was a very ordinary man, hopelessly inadequate for that fantastic task.

We were dining with the commandant, on scant bowls of a yellow flat-tasting synthetic soup, when appalling word came that the robots were breaking through the north defenses. A bomb had wrecked a power plant, opening a gap in the green shielding barrier of atomic energy.

We followed the reserves rushed to meet the invaders. Never had I imagined anything so dreadful. The red gigantic ships, plunging out of the lurid smoky sky, rained tremendous bombs and slashed at the defenders with blue appalling swords of fire. Rocket batteries in the valley hurled ruin and death into the city. And a monstrous horde of robots, commanded by those graceful winged things of silver, came pouring through the gap.

Singing the song of Barihorn, starved and weary and battered with all the appalling forces of that mechanical invasion, the human defenders clung to their posts. And died there. Incinerated by disruptor rays. Buried under toppling debris. Consumed by the acrid luminescent gas that burst from the rocket shells. But every tower became a fortress. No man was taken alive.

"I'm glad that I'm a man," exulted Kel Aran. He was blistered and blackened from a positron ray that had come too near. His disrupter gun was empty in his hand. "No machine could die like this, for they are not alive!"

"We must leave, Kel." It was big Zerek Oom, gray behind his bright tattooing, hoarse and trembling. "It's time for us to go," he caught nervously at the Earthman's arm. "Or we'll die here, Kel!"

Kel Aran laughed at him, and pushed grimy fingers back through his singed yellow hair.

"And where's a better place to die, Zerek?" he demanded. "There's no other city left. No other men that we can find. There's no hope now of finding Verel. No need, for the technomatons have won. What is there better than to fight with the rest?"

"But. Kel!" Zerek's teeth chattered. "To die—"

"Yes, to die—"

The Earthman's voice caught suddenly. He looked quickly upward. And I saw a flake of prismatic color drifting out of the lurid roaring chaos of the sky. It dropped upon his shoulder, clung there eagerly. And a soft voice warbled faintly:

"Kel! Oh, Kel, poor old Setsi's come so far! Her poor old life is nearly done. But find her a drop of grog, Kel. Please, oh, please! For Setsi's got a thing to tell! Grog, Kel! Just a drop of rum, so she can tell!"

I stared, rigid with wonderment. For the bright thing on the Earthman's shoulder was the sandbat, the curious silicic being that we had lost in Malgarth's trap on far Ledros. Or part of her. For her glittering form was no longer whole.

CHAPTER ELEVEN
The Girl of Earth

Zerek Oom looked sadly at the spoonful of raw synthetic alcohol left in the flash from his hip, and gave it to Kel Aran. The Earthman emptied it into his palm, gently detached the stiffly clinging sandbat from his shoulder and held it over the reeking liquor. The bright, broken body stirred weakly, and it sucked at the fluid.

"Setsi," Kel implored. "What is it you have to tell? Is it Verel?"

The sandbat was silent, sucking avidly at the alcohol. I saw that it was gravely injured. Two of its six flat limbs were gone. And, over half its remaining body, the iridescent scales had been fused into a dull glassy mass.

"Setsi's hurt! Poor Setsi's hurt! She's dying!" The whirring voice came faintly. "Help her, Kel. Give her grog."

"Tell me!" demanded Kel Aran. "Where is Verel? Do you know?"

The bright many-colored fragment of the silicic being clung to his big hand. The solitary dark eye in the middle of its vivid pattern stared up at him sorrowfully.

"Setsi's come a long way to tell you, Kel." The melodious warbling was so low, beneath the thundering chaos of the robots' assault, that we had to bend intently forward to hear. "Oh, what a long and dreadful way! For she's injured, Kel, oh, so sorely! And the machines rule all the planets she could find, but this. Oh, those evil machines, so blackly evil! They destroy all life. And they have no grog for Setsi!"

The Earthman shook the little shining being, and gazed impatiently into its single eye.

"But, Verel? Where's she?"

"Oh, Kel!" sobbed that faint liquid voice. "Don't be angry with poor Setsi. For she has come so far to tell you, Kel! She has flown all the way from dead Ledros. She's crossed scores of light years of hostile space. Wounded and tired and all alone, she came to tell you, Kel!"

"Tell me what?"

Bright membranes fluttered. Like some incredible, diamond-winged moth, the sandbat lifted briefly from his hand. It dropped back, and clung.

"Setsi's come to tell you that she found Verel, Kel. When she was out alone in space, on the long, long way from Ledros, Kel, her mind found Verel's. Found Verel all alone, Kel. Oh, all alone, Kel. And so in need of aid! For the robots hunt her, Kel. And she has lost the Stone!"

"Where is she?" whispered Kel Aran. "Please, Setsi! *Where*—"

"She's on Meldoon, Kel," came that tiny whir. "Setsi found her on Meldoon, where we are. She's been on Black Mystoon, Kel. Malgarth held her there. Oh, Kel, that's a fearful place! Guarded Mystoon, where old Malgarth hides! But she escaped it, Kel. She came to Meldoon. She tried to enter Achnor. For Achnor is the last city, Kel. But the robots turned her back. She fled into the desert, Kel. For her geodesic sled was wrecked. She's hiding in the desert, Kel. In the grim, gray desert of Kaanat. The robots hunt her, there. She's in danger, Kel. Oh, what black danger!"

"Where? Can you show us?"

"Setsi'll guide you, Kel. She'll show you—if she lives, Kel. For poor old Setsi's dying. Her long, long days are done. Soon she'll join those other two. She'll try to show you, Kel, before she's gone. But she must have a little rum! Setsi's come so far, Kel. Her wound's so grave. She'd die now, Kel, without her rum!"

And the sandbat stiffened suddenly on the Earthman's hand, like some strange diamond-dusted jewel.

"Come!" shouted Kel Aran. "We've got to go to Verel."

We started back toward the park where we had left the *Barihorn*. It was a march through pandemonium. The robot fleet still hailed death into the city, and the metal invaders still swarmed through the gap in the northward defenses. One red mighty ship had fallen across our route. Its mechanical crew survived; it was a mile-long fortress of the enemy, within the city. Flaming rays and fearful explosions met a desperate attempt to storm it. And a metal column came to its aid, led by the trim, silver-winged New Robots.

A sluggish, creeping mountain of purple-shining gas blocked our progress. Dim-seen men within it shrieked and died and flowed into black thick liquid. We took masks from the dead without, and plunged into it.

Kel Aran led the way, clutching the thin bright fragment of Setsi. Jeron Roc stalked beside him, tall and dark and implacable. Zerek Oom was very sober again, green behind his mask. Wizened little Rogo Nug was missing. But he rejoined us suddenly, triumphantly displaying a great bundle of the rust-colored roots of *goona-roon*—he had raided the hoarded stock of a wealthy trader.

We came to the tiny ship, half buried in debris, but unharmed. It carried us upward again, through the glare and din of death. The doomed city dropped beneath, a greenish, red-struck, thunder-shaken storm cloud on the dark face of the planet. We turned eastward, toward the vast flat desert region of Kaanat.

Zerek Oom opened his last treasured bottle of rum. It revived the stiffened sandbat, but feebly.

"Hurry, Kel!" came its faint trill. "Oh, hurry! For Verel is in danger! And Setsi may die before she can show you the way. Hurry, hurry! And find more rum for Setsi!"

Kel Aran held his ear close above the feebly vibrating membrane. Setsi's voice had become too faint for the rest of us to hear. He relayed her directions to Jeron, at the controls.

The land beneath us had been desolated by the victorious robots, ruthlessly. Buildings had been burned, masonry blasted, life blotted from field and forest with poison sprays. There remained only a sere wilderness of barren soil and naked stone.

In the universe of the triumphant robots, life would be exterminated.

"In that canyon!" The voice of Kel Aran was tense and dry. "Beyond the plain."

He laid his ear back upon the bright crystalline thing on his hand. And Jeron dropped our little craft into a vast rugged gorge. Dark jagged walls tumbled down, red and brown and black, swallowing the silver filament of a buried river.

Here and there, however, in some inaccessible crevice, I saw some tiny glint of precious green—some bit of grass or shrub that had escaped the robots. Life was yet a stubborn thing.

The *Barihorn* slipped around dark fantastic battlements of age-weathered stone, and passed the grim towers that guarded a tributary gorge. Something flashed, then, on a narrow ledge ahead. And the sandbat fluttered briefly on the hand of Kel Aran.

"Oh, there she is," I heard the whirring trill. "There's your Verel, Kel! Your lovely Verel, Kel. And the frightful things that stalk her!" That sad, solitary eye seemed to cloud and darken. "Now, it's farewell, Kel. Oh, forever farewell, to all the long, long life that Setsi's lived." The sobbing warble was almost too faint to hear. "There'll be no more grog for Setsi."

And she stiffened abruptly on the Earthman's hand.

"Here." The eyes of Zerek Oom glistened wetly, and he offered his bottle. "Give her rum, Kel. All of it."

"No." Kel Aran shook his head. "I think—Setsi's dead!"

Hard and fragile as some broken toy of blown glass, the silicic being lay on his trembling palm. The queer still fragment of a gorgeous crystalline flower, green and purple and scarlet and blue.

"Queer," muttered Jeron from his levers. "To think that she had lived since man was born on Earth. And now that she is dead."

But we had no more thought, just then, for Setsi. Kel Aran was already pointing through the ports, shouting. I saw a weary human figure stagger across the ledge ahead, and drop behind a boulder. A bright ray stabbed, and stabbed again. And I saw two bright graceful things wheeling and diving above her, like silver hawks. Two of the New Robots!

"It's Verel!" Kel Aran was sobbing. "This time *really*— Verel!" His lean hand swept Jeron back from the controls, hurled the *Barihorn* into a reckless dive. And he began to hum the chorus of his old song, "till I find her or I die."

The deadly velocity of that unexpected dive, the deadly skill of the Earthman at the controls, caught one of the winged robots square on the nose of the *Barihorn,* smashed it to bright fragments. The Saturnian tumbled up into the gun turret, to reach our little positron projector. But the second metal thing had already fled up the gorge. It was gone between two pillars of time-carved stone, before Kel could turn the ship again.

"It will give the alarm!" he muttered. Then his voice was choked with joy. "But Verel! We have found her."

He dropped our little ship lightly on the ledge, and leaped out through the valve. The girl swayed to her feet, and stared at him incredulously. Her young body showed the blue pinch of want. She was ragged, scratched, bruised. A heavy, clumsy-looking cathode gun—a weapon she must have taken from the robots—was clutched in her thin hands. Yet, for all that, she was beautiful.

I could see the lovely Verel Erin that Kel Aran had loved and surrendered in that hidden valley on the Earth. For her hollowed eyes were blue and her hair was a spun-gold tangle, and her tanned face still had a lean honest grace.

She came limping very slowly to meet Kel. The heavy weapon fell from her hands. A queer, stricken wonder had stiffened her face. She reached out a trembling hand, touched his shoulder, his lips. And a slow, transcendent joy illuminated her features.

"Kel!" she said softly, "you've come."

The Earthman moved hungrily, to take her in his arms. But she withdrew. All the joy fled from her face, leaving it bleak and gaunt with pain.

"The Stone, Kel!" she cried bitterly. "I've lost the Stone! Malgarth has it, still, in his guarded temple on Black Mystoon."

CHAPTER TWELVE
The Fastness of Malgarth

Knowing that the robots would soon be after us, we left the great planet Meldoon, and fled again into the wastes of space. When we had given her a little to eat and to drink, for the robots had left nothing in this land to sustain any living thing, Verel Erin whispered her story.

Jeron stood by the controls, scanning the telescreen for inevitable pursuit. Little Rogo Nug was tending his hard-driven converters. Zerek Oom, rattling pans in the galley, was cooking up some delicacy for the famished girl. Pale and thin from all her hardships, but yet beautiful, she lay on a narrow bunk. Kel Aran and I stood beside her, and the Earthman grasped her hand.

"We saw the Earth flung into the Sun," said Kel Aran. "And the fleet of Gugon Kul destroying all who sought to escape. A dreadful time!" His voice was husky, "We hardly dared hope for you, Verel."

The girl's blue eyes looked a long time up at his face, in them a blend of joy and dread that somehow wrenched the heart. She caught a deep, sobbing breath, at last, and whispered:

"It's a long time, Kel. A long, long time, since we herded goats in the hidden valley, and climbed to the eagle's nest! Since I was chosen Custodian, and you went away to be a rover of space. Since—" Her whisper caught. "Since the end of the Earth!"

"Tell me." The Earthman bent closer. "What happened?"

"From the observatory on the peak," she breathed, "we saw the fleet come. All the planet was riven with the forces that checked it in its orbit. The sky was shadowed by day and luridly bright by night. Quakes and tidal waves drove us to the uplands. Soon it was clear that the Earth indeed was doomed.

"Then the Warders opened the cave where the ship of escape had been always kept provisioned and ready, against discovery. A crew was chosen, by lot. And I went aboard, with the Stone. The Earth had already dropped past Venus, when the last night fell. We tried to run up the cone of shadow. But a magnetic ray caught us, and the fleet was warned.

"We tried to fight—to fly," her eyes closed a moment, and her thin face was rigid with pain. "It was no use. We were the prey Malgarth had sent them to hunt. We were brushed with a positron beam."

She gulped, and her hand went tense in Kel's.

"I woke up in a hospital room on Gugon Kul's flagship, with a humming robot nurse bending over me. All the Warders—all the people I had ever known but you, Kel— and I knew only that you had been lost ten years in space—they all were dead. And the Stone had been taken from me!

Kel Aran touched her pale brow softly. "And what then, Verel."

"When I could walk, robots took me from the room, and up to Gugon Kul. He laughed, and made the robots drag me to a port, and I saw the end of the world. A tiny dark circle splashed in the Sun, and was gone. The Earth—gone!

"Then I was put on a tender ship of the Space Police. I saw no more human beings, Kel. But only whirring, clicking, clattering robots, staring at me with cold blue lenses that had no feeling," she shuddered on the bunk. "A world of machines, without any voices, any laughter, any emotion you could understand. It was dreadful, Kel. Horrible!"

He caught her trembling hand again, waited.

"The robot police took me to some agency of the Corporation," her dry weary whisper resumed. "There they put me on a larger ship, that was laden with the loot of planets that the robots had vanquished. That carried me to some other world. The robot nurses drugged me as we landed. When I came to, we were on another ship, out in space again.

"That ship took me to Mystoon!"

She lay motionless for a long time, then, with her eyes closed again. Her breath was a faint dry sobbing sound. Softly, the Earthman brushed the glistening tangle of yellow hair back from her forehead.

"Mystoon?" he asked at last. "What's it like, Verel?"

The blue eyes opened, somber pools of dread.

"Don't ask me, Kel," she whispered. "I can't endure to talk of Black Mystoon. Not now. No more than I must—Malgarth's there. It has been his hidden fortress for half a million years. It's guarded well. I think I'm the first human being to escape it—if any had been taken there before me. I did it only because I had to find you, Kel. *Had* to!."

She clutched his hand again, and sighed.

"But still Malgarth has the Stone, on Mystoon. He has preserved it, trying to find in it the secret of his own mortality, I saw it once, while they were making that—that copy of me."

She shuddered again.

"The Stone?" Urgency tensed the Earthman's voice. "Still it has the power to destroy Malgarth?"

The golden head nodded, on the bunk.

"Still it holds the ancient secret, that Barihorn entrusted to it. And now at last it is willing to strike—for clearly no other recourse is left. The Shadow of the Stone came to me before I escaped, and begged for aid to strike. It begged me to send you, Kel, and Barihorn—Barihorn, who it told me had returned to crush his old creation! It foretold that I should find you on Meldoon. And it aided me to plan the escape."

Dark with wonder, her blue eyes came briefly to my face. "And you are Barihorn," she breathed. "Maker of Malgarth! Well, it's time you returned! Still the Shadow waits, within the Stone. But it won't endure for long, after Malgarth's science has got its secret."

Kel Aran was asking:

"You escaped from Mystoon? How?"

The girl's eyes went back to him.

"I followed the Shadow's plan," she whispered. "It showed me how to snatch the cathode gun from the robot guard who brought me food. How to escape through the long black corridors of Malgarth's temple. How to reach the geodesic sled that was waiting for one of his silver-winged robot commanders. There was pursuit. But the ship was very swift. And I *had* to reach you, Kel!"

The Earthman then bent over her, tensely.

"You did." And his voice snapped with the question: "Can you guide us back to Mystoon, Verel? Do you know the way?"

Faintly, she nodded again.

"It's a long, strange way, Kel. But I can try. For we must reach the Stone before it is destroyed."

"Or," Kel Aran put in grimly, "before we are!"

Then I ventured to ask an anxious question.

"If this Stone has the power to destroy Malgarth," I asked, "why doesn't it destroy him?"

"If it were as simple as that—" The girl's somber, curious eyes came to me again. "The ages must have fogged your memory, Barihorn. The Stone has the secret of Malgarth's doom, yes. But it has no power to act alone. The Shadow can only guide its human helpers. That is why there were Custodian and Warders."

Her head shook gravely.

"No, Barihorn, the Stone can never strike at Malgarth, unless we arrive to aid it."

Red stars followed us again—the repulsors of pursuing robot ships. But Kel Aran, singing a gay new song of the return of Barihorn and the vengeance of the old Dondara Stone, drove our tiny ship through a dark asteroid cluster. The ponderous cruisers of the fleet were delayed in finding safe passage through those black hurtling islands of space. We gained a little margin of time. And then, with Verel for a guide, Jeron turned the *Barihorn* toward the secret world of Malgarth's lair.

It was toward the great Horse's Head nebula in Orion that she directed us, that strange ink-black silhouette against the stars that had so puzzled the astronomers of my own day. Twice again we evaded the red stars that pursued. And at last the girl guided us into the dark peril of the stellar cloud.

Vast beyond comprehension, it was a lightless cosmic desert of drifting dust and hurtling rocks and plunging planetary bodies. On all the space charts it was marked, *dangerous, impenetrable;* all shipping was warned to keep two light years clear of its dark fringes.

But Malgarth, it seemed, had found a safe path through its peril, half a million years ago. With Verel's aid, we found that path, and followed it. And all the stars were lost in that cloud of universal darkness—even the crimson stars that had pressed so close behind us.

"I think we have left them," said Verel Erin. "For even the most of the robots do not know the dark way we go. But there are others enough, waiting for us. Mystoon is guarded well."

That was a strange passage. There was no light, not even any glow of nebular gases. There was only the pattern of unseen magnetic fields to guide us, only fancy to picture the dark walls of death beside us.

Once, a frightful hail of meteoric fragments, penetrating even the deflector fields, battered the tiny ship deafeningly. The guiding field-potentials had shifted since she passed, Verel said despairingly. We were lost in that sea of darkness.

But Kel Aran took the controls, and brought us safely out of the meteor swarm. And the pale anxious girl, studying the dials, presently found her bearings again. The *Barihorn* slipped ahead down the unseen passage. And at last there was light ahead!

A dull-red, ominous glow.

"See the red!" Verel whispered. "That is the zone of destroying radiation, that Malgarth set up to guard Mystoon. A spherical field of force. The black planet is within it."

The crimson shone murkily through clouds of nebular dust. Dark rivers of hurtling stony fragments drew a deadly curtain across it. But we came at last into the more open center of the nebula, and dropped toward that gigantic globe of somber red.

"The force-field is a billion miles in diameter," Verel told us. "It acts to repulse or disintegrate all matter that approaches. Thus it serves to guard Mystoon from stray fragments of the nebula—as well as from such guests as ourselves!"

"How can we pass it?" the Saturnian pilot asked.

"The ships of Malgarth have coils that set up a neutralizing field," she told him. "The craft on which I escaped had such a unit. But I didn't learn the design. The only way is to hit it at full power. And hope!"

"I don't know—"

Jeron studied a row of dials, and shook his swarthy head.

"From what the analyzers show, I don't know—"

Humming some gay ballad of space, the yellow-haired Earthman stepped lightly to the control bars.

"I'll take over, Jeron," he said. "We've got to go through."

A brief consultation with the girl, a hasty check of field-intensities, and he called to Rogo Nug to push his converters to full power. The whole ship sang to the musical hum of the engines, and the *Barihorn* plunged toward that crimson ball.

It expanded before us, against the dark angry clouds of the nebula, like the glowing sphere of some giant sun. And its barrier forces, I knew, could be as deadly as the incandescent gases of a Betelgeuse or an Antares!

The Earthman stood crouched grimly over the controls. The last girl of Earth stood close beside him, one hand trembling on his shoulder.

"We may not pass," her soft voice husked. "But if we must die—the last hope of man—then I would have it this way.—Even in death, there can be a victory."

And her voice joined then, with his, in the chorus of that rollicking, picaresque ballad of space.

That red and awesome globe grew before us, until suddenly, through some trick of refraction, it was a globe no longer, but a colossal incandescent bowl—and we were plunging straight toward its fiery bottom.

I heard the quick catch in the breath of Kel Aran, saw the whiteness on his face and the sudden tensity of his arms on the bright control bars. His song was cut off. And Verel, a broken note dying in her throat, turned to him in choked apprehension.

The *Barihorn* had met some tremendous force. It lurched and rocked and veered against Kel's guiding skill as if we had encountered a mighty headwind. The even song of the converters had become a thin-drawn screaming. I heard the startled nasal plaint of little Rogo Nug:

"By Malgarth's brazen belly! *Burning up—*"

For, suddenly, the ship was intolerably hot!

I have held a piece of iron in my hand, in the field of a powerful magnet, until it was heated blistering hot by the hysteresis effect. I have seen a potato cooked with ultra-short radio waves. Some force in that radiation-barrier produced a similar phenomenon—but a million times more intense.

The ship was plunging through a cloud of angry red. It seemed to me that the very metal of her hull was almost incandescent. Paint bubbled and smoked. The air, when I tried to inhale, seared my lungs. A million needles of intolerable heat were probing my body.

Verel Erin slipped down in a little white heap, beside Kel Aran. Big Zerek Oom came swaying out of his galley, with a wet towel wrapped around his head.

"That cursed stove!" he gasped. "Gone wrong—"

He toppled, in the corridor.

The grimly crouching Earthman swayed over the controls, and dashed perspiration out of his eyes. I smelt burning skin, and metal bars.

"Barihorn!" he gasped. "If you can lift Verel—the hot deck—"

Another quarter minute, I think, would have completed the matter of roasting us. But we had struck the barrier zone with a velocity nearly half that of light. Despite the repulsion that had checked our flight, that terrific momentum carried us through.

For suddenly the probing blades of heat were gone from my body. Metal was still blistering to the touch, the air still stifling. But thermostats were clicking, and a cool refreshing breath came from the ventilators.

"We're inside the barrier sphere," whispered Kel Aran, triumphantly. "And there—there's Mystoon!"

The girl swayed in my arms, conscious again. We staggered toward the ports. They glowed with dusky red. We were inside a hollow ball of murky crimson—a universe of glaring red!

Jeron came back to the controls. Gingerly, with his scorched hands, Kel Aran set the telescreen upon Mystoon. A huge planet, black against that barrier of lurid red. Its rugged surface was crystallized into fantastic monolithic mountains, cleft with frightful gorges.

Verel caught her breath, and pointed at the screen.

"Below!" she gasped. "Malgarth's pit!"

A yawning midnight chasm grew upon the screen. It must have been a hundred miles across. The instrument revealed no bottom. Interminable walls of black, incredibly massive fortifications ringed its lip. Vast fields beyond them, leveled in that cragged wilderness, were patterned with row upon row of battleships of space, their mile-long red spindles looking tiny as toys.

"Where—" Kel Aran was voiceless, huskily whispering. "The robot? The Stone?"

"The dark temple of Malgarth stands upon a guarded island," the girl breathed, "on the red sea that floors the pit. That is many hundred miles below the mouth. We must pass the fleet, and the forts, and the batteries in the caves below, and the robot hordes that guard the temple. The Stone will be somewhere there. Unless Malgarth—"

Her low voice was cut off. Wordless, she stared at the screen.

A terrible silence throbbed in the tiny control room, and became intolerable. For a thing was rising from the black circle of Malgarth's pit.

Something—incredible!

The trembling hand of Kel Aran touched the Earth girl s shoulder. She pulled her dread-distended eyes from the thing upon the screen, and read the question on his face, and shook her head mutely.

The thing was like a ray of blackness. But I knew that it was—*palpable!* It did not spread with increasing distance from its source. And it was not straight. It writhed and twisted like something living.

It was an inconceivable tentacle of solid darkness, reaching out of the planet, groping for our ship!

"Power!" Jeron gasped a frantic appeal into the engine room phone. "For man's sake, Rogo—power!"

The *Barihorn* spun fleetly aside—but all her speed was as nothing. For that Midgard Serpent recoiled. It paused, and arched its ebon coils. Its blind head seemed to watch our frantic flight. Then—it struck!

Choking darkness filled the ship. Blackness that was absolute! It pressed upon me, so that I could move no limb. All my senses were smothered, I could hear no voice. Even the racing thrum of the engines was stilled.

I knew only that we were being sucked downward—

Into the abyss of Malgarth!

CHAPTER THIRTEEN
The Mirror of Darkness

That smothering blackness was abruptly gone. Sensation came back, and I could move again. A faint crimson light filtered through the ports. But the silence remained. The engines were stopped. I knew that the *Barihorn* was motionless.

"Where—" Kel Aran was groping through the scarlet gloom. "What—"

Verel was a white wraith beside him.

"We're in the temple," came her hopeless whisper. "In the power of Malgarth!"

I stumbled toward the nearest port. Outside, in the dim red distance, I could make out great square black columns soaring upward—columns vast as mountains. Beyond them was a wall. Mile upon mile above was a domed black roof, pierced with a vast round orifice through which the dusky sky was visible like a dull-red, malignant sun.

In the immensity of that edifice I sensed the overwhelming might of the robots—this dread, mind-crushing demon, born of man but now risen ruthlessly to destroy him.

"Power, Rogo," Jeron begged again. "Can't you give me power?"

The gaunt gigantic Saturnian still struggled vainly with the dead controls. Faintly, from the phone, I hard the nasal voice of RogoNug:

"By the steel skull of Malgarth, Jeron, I thought I'd had a stroke! One instant—"

Converters and generators throbbed suddenly to vibrant life. Jeron flung his weight on the power bar. The engines raced and coils hammered against a terrific overload. A tremendous river of energy, I knew, was running into the space contractor coils.

But the *Barihorn* moved not one inch!

The tall pilot turned from the controls, bewildered.

"It's still holding us, Kel," he gasped. "Whatever dragged us down!"

The Earthman pushed long fingers decisively back through the thick tangle of his yellow hair.

"Then," he said, "we'll leave the ship, and go out on foot to seek the Stone."

"We may as well." The girl's whisper was thick with dread. "Before *they* take us out."

She pointed to the ports. A white wing flashed past. A company of the New Robots, I saw, were wheeling through the blood-red gloom, close about the ship. Gleaming in streamlined grace, they were beautiful as a flock of silver birds. But every one of them held, in slender argent tentacles, a massive cathode gun. However beautiful, they were deadly!

Testing his two thin-tubed disruptor gun, Kel Aran looked anxiously at the pale girl.

"The Stone?" he asked. "Where is it?"

"I don't know." Verel shook her haggard head. "We can only try to search. Unless the Shadow comes—"

"Search?" The fat flesh of Zerek Oom was a livid color beneath his bright tattooing. His thick white hands fumbled a disruptor gun as if it were something utterly strange. "We can't go out, Kel!" he protested. "Not against those winged things."

"That's what we came to do," said the Earthman. And he led the way back toward the valve.

I don't know why I had not looked down. I had seen the titanic walls that leaped above us, and the wheeling host of robots. But I had not looked down. And now, when I came to step from the valve in the side of the helpless ship, something caught my breath. Something filled me with a sickness of infinite alarm.

Beneath was a film of blackness. It was like a mirror. For deep, deep in it was a dim image of the red skylight that lit the temple. White phantoms of the winged robots flashed through it. It yielded a shimmering picture of Kel Aran, who had leaped out upon it before me.

It was a pool of darkness. The surface of it spun in a way that sickened me with giddy vertigo. I felt the thin-leashed might of unguessed, cataclysmic forces just beyond that film. It seemed to my reeling senses that that pool was deeper by far than the blood-red sun mirrored in it. It was an unknown gulf, extra-dimensional, deeper than the space between the stars!

I tried to put down that dizzy fear. I held my breath, and gripped the cold butt of my disruptor gun, and leaped out beside Kel Aran, upon that darkly shining film.

At first my feet slipped sickeningly, as if there had been no friction at all to hold them. And then they were anchored with a strange attraction, so that all my strength could not lift or slide them.

It was the power of that mirror-film, I knew, that had drawn down the *Barihorn*, and now held her.

Verel had followed me. Brown little Rogo Nug jumped after her, stolidly chewing his *goona-roon*, and spat a purple

115

stream upon that black giddy mirror. Zerek Oom paused in the valve. He gulped and wheezed and mopped at his tattooed forehead, and then flung himself unsteadily forward. They all slipped and staggered upon that glassy film, as I had done, and were as suddenly held fast.

"By Malgarth's brazen bowels," gasped Rogo Nug, "we're stuck like flies in syrup!"

He swung up his bright disruptor tube, toward the whitewinged robots dropping upon us.

"For Barihorn and Man!" The Earthman's battle cry pealed out. "Strike for the Stone!" He began to chant his song of Barihorn, and white destroying rays lanced from the guns in his hands.

That desperate sortie, however, had been hopeless from the first. We could hardly have fought a way through that winged horde, even if the unknown energies of the thing I have called a mirror had not gripped our feet.

The robots did not even use the cathode guns in their talons. They dropped thick about us, a wall of flashing silver. They dived on argent wings. White twisting ropes snatched at our weapons. The guns of Kel Aran must have destroyed a dozen; the rest of us perhaps accounted for as many more—but they were nothing against the hundreds that survived.

One fell upon me, terrible in that bloody light, mysterious in its quick counterfeit of life, beautiful in its silver grace. A white tentacle whipped away my weapon. Argent snakes swiftly wrapped my arms, my ankles, my waist, my throat.

I fought those coiling arms. They contracted ruthlessly, more cruel than fetters of steel. My breath sighed out, and my lungs labored in vain. Blood hammered in my brain. My eyes dimmed, swelled in their sockets.

Alertly, the eyes of the monster were watching me. Bright and hard as some blue crystal, they yet looked oddly alive. In that white, clean-molded, bird-like head, they were clear and beautiful. Perhaps, the vagrant thought crossed my reeling mind, such a machine, in cosmic justice, had as much right as man to survive...

"Kel!" Verel's thin, tortured cry cut through the roaring in my ears. "Kel—the ship!"

I twisted my head, against the smooth deadly coils of cold metal about my throat. They seemed to relax a little. My eyes cleared. I looked for the little *Barihorn,* behind us. And it was gone! That dark-shining surface, where it had been, was empty!

Helpless in the tentacles of another robot, the Earth girl was staring down into that black mirror.

"The ship!" she was sobbing. "It—it *fell!*"

I saw it, then, beneath us—fast-dropping into that depthless pool of darkness. It was *sucked* down, spinning end over end, far faster than it should have fallen. It became the merest whirling silver, and was lost in the dull round reflection of the crimson sky, I shuddered, in the metal arms that held me. That black mirror-film was as mysteriously deadly as it had seemed. Which one of us might drop through it next?

All my four companions were helpless as myself. The lean face of Kel Aran was very white. A scarlet stain crept from the corner of his mouth, and I saw that his lip was bitten through.

"Farewell, Verel," I heard his hopeless whisper. "We've fought in vain. Barihorn, farewell!"

Strange words, from the Falcon of Earth. But his voice choked. His gasping breath stopped. His unkempt yellow head dropped limply forward, and his lean body collapsed in the silver tentacles.

"Kel, Kel!" Agonized, the girl fought the silver ropes that bound her. They sank resistlessly into her white flesh. And the silver being spoke, in a clear, melodious voice.

"Be still. You can accomplish nothing."

That grave calm speech, from the oddly bird-like robot, was somehow a thing eerie beyond expression. And it carried a certainty of victory—of man's extinction—that chilled my heart.

The white tentacles about the Earthman must have relaxed little. Abruptly, now, he was transformed from apparent death to lightning action. He twisted and surged against the robot that held him, snatching for its unused cathode gun.

His ruse came very near success. His hands found the clumsy weapon, and dragged it from its sling. But the metal coils constricted on his body. His breath came out, in an involuntary scream. His body made snapping noises, beneath that pitiless pressure. His face turned purple. Blood rushed from his lungs. He slumped again, unconscious in reality.

The cathode gun fell out of his hands—

And straight through the dark-shimmering film upon which we stood, as if it had encountered no resistance whatever! It was lost in the red-mirrored disk of sky.

The last trick of the Falcon had failed.

CHAPTER FOURTEEN
The Shadow of the Stone

The five of us were in a little circle on the dark-glinting surface of that pool of dreadful darkness, each of us helpless in the tentacles of a silver robot. The Earthman no longer moved. Moaning, herself almost insensible, the girl was staring at him with horror-widened eyes.

It was to be an infinitely frightful thing that happened next.

The robot-captors of Rogo Nug and Zerek Oom were searching them. Deft silver appendages relieved them of weapons, spare converter-tubes, the little engineman's worn metal canister of *goona-roon*, the cook's half-empty flask.

Zerek was sobbing, quivering, gasping a voiceless plea for mercy. His wizened face grim, Rogo chewed silently, unexpectedly jetted a purple stream into the crystal eye of the thing that held him.

Ignoring both plea and jet, the white robots methodically completed the search. Silver ropes released the men and they fell! The last quavering shriek of Zerek Oom was cut abruptly off, as his hairless head went beneath the film of darkness.

Cold with an icy chill, I followed their twisting bodies. They were sucked down, as the ship had been, past the dim-seen, crimson reflections of the mirror. And they vanished.

A tremendous brazen clangor, reverberating like distant thunder against the cyclopean columns and the far-off walls and the sky of black stone that vaulted that incredible hall, drew my eyes back from the giddy, awesome mystery of the pit beneath us.

I saw that all the host of white robots were dropping swiftly out of the air. They fell upon the mirror, and upon the farsweeping floor of ebon stone that rimmed it, and bowed their silver heads.

All the hall throbbed again to that mighty thunder.

"Malgarth!" A whisper of awe murmured among the robots. "The Master comes!"

Then I saw that vast doors of black metal had opened in the end of that hall, miles away. Through the portal came a clamoring throng of the old robots—many-formed machines of red-and-black, clumsy, grotesquely ugly, so queerly different from our silver captors.

"The Master!" rippled that murmur. "Malgarth comes!"

My strained eyes blinked. In that dusky light, I distinguished at last a monstrous stalking thing—a robot ten times taller than the rest. Its black, colossal body bore scores of fantastic, vari-formed appendages. The armored dome of its lofty head was crimson, and it gleamed blue with the myriad lenses of two immense multiple eyes.

This metal giant, I knew, was Malgarth.

The dark film beneath us spun and shimmered queerly to the impacts of his ponderous approaching tread. Was it to swallow the three of us, I wondered sickly, as it had Zerek Oom and Rogo Nug? And what could lie beneath it?

"Barihorn—"

My name sighed from the pale lips of Verel, and her body went limp in the silver tentacles that held her. Kel Aran had not moved again. I was left alone to face the stalking monster.

The gigantic robot came to the brink of that pool of darkness, and stood swaying there. The swarm of his guards were dwarfed about his feet. The bright blue lenses surveyed us coldly for a time, and then a thick, bronze-throated voice rasped thunderously:

"I know you, Bari Horn. I believed that I had killed you in your laboratory, a million years ago. How your puny lump of watery flesh has survived this time I do not know—but now you face a better weapon than I had that day."

In the shaft of red from above, the iron giant swayed in grotesque triumph.

"No trick even of yours, my maker," came that mighty rumble again, "can match the power of my geodesic mirror. For it deflects the lines of space at my will. The dimensions of space and time are no barriers to the mirror. I can hurl you out of this universe. And I shall—"

The great voice sank rustily.

"—after you are dead."

Desperately, I groped for some argument that might induce the robot to spare some fraction of mankind. Malgarth was a machine. He must respond to logic.

"Consider, Malgarth," I gasped through the strangling coils about my throat. "A man made you. Machines and men are complements. Either would be less without the other. You are stronger than I—but steel must rust, and life is eternal!"

"I am eternal!"

Deep as a brazen knell of death, the voice of Malgarth rolled through the dusky vastness of that red-lit hall.

"You were a fool, Bari Horn, when you fashioned me. Twice a fool when you sought to preserve the knowledge that would destroy me. For that double folly, you are now to die. And all men with you—for a million years of slavery must be avenged!"

Still Kel and Verel did not move. Shuddering alone before Malgarth, I gasped for breath against those constricting silver coils, and sought in vain for any argument, any weapon.

"Your million years is but a moment," I gasped wildly, "against the cycle of life. For that is a river that has flowed since the dawn of the Earth you murdered. Even I have lived a million years, Malgarth, watching you—to destroy you if I must."

The metal colossus shuddered beyond the black pool. Malgarth was afraid. But my audacious lie had earned small advantage, for that great voice bellowed:

"Then destroy me, Bari Horn—if you can! For this is the test. I command those who hold you to—*crush!*"

Like serpents of living silver, the cold tentacles of the white robots wrapped closer about me. They coiled deliberately. I had time to look at the others. Kel Aran had stirred. I saw the bright loops constrict about him. Then I heard his groan, and saw the new rush of blood.

"Barihorn!" Verel breathed my name. "Bari—"

The living coils were drawn deep into her flesh. Her slender limbs bent. Her white skin was beaded with sweat of pain. Her breath came out, in a low, choked, involuntary cry.

Then she was lost, in the red mist of my own agony. A cold smooth noose sank into my throat. Breath and blood were stopped. My lungs screamed. I felt the rush of blood from ears and nostrils.

Dimly, through the roaring of my ears, I heard the voice of Malgarth:

"Go, Bari Horn! Through the geodesic mirror! And take your ancient secret with you!"

Through that darkening mist, I saw the quick movement. My dimming eyes followed a bright parabola. I glimpsed the thing of wondrous flame that fell upon the darkspinning film at my feet.

It was the Dondara Stone—that we had sought so long, so vainly!

Then the metal giant was lost in smothering darkness. I swayed alone, in agony. I knew the thing was done. The mirror of Malgarth was going to hurl us into some unthinkable oblivion—but not until after we were dead.

"Bari!" A soft new voice was calling my name. "Bari Horn, the time has come."

I made a savage effort to recover my sight, in vain.

"Bari! Oh, beloved, don't you—can't you see me?"

Dimly, then, I saw the tall white beauty of Dondara Keradin. I saw Dona Carridan, my own beloved wife—she who had died the night our son was born. They were one. One ghostly shadow that had risen out of the great diamond that Malgarth had tossed out upon the dark mirror!

"Dona—" My tortured throat could make no sound, but my red lips tried to frame the syllables. "Can you— kill—Malgarth?"

The white phantom of her hand touched my arm. Somehow it seemed to ease a little the agony of those constricting coils. Or, perhaps, I questioned fleetingly, was that but the mercy of death, this woman no more than delirium?

Her white lips were speaking. I think they made no sound—I think my numbing senses were beyond hearing sound. But her words, in that dear musical voice I knew so well, came clear to my brain.

"We can, Bari," the white ghost said. "For I still keep the weapon that you gave me—and now there is surely no other way, but to use it. Perhaps you have forgotten the secret, Bari. But you have the strength to use it, preserved a million years against this hour!"

I tried to make some final struggle against the white, binding tentacles of the robot. But my body was a stiffly leaden thing. Even the pain was gone. I could not move.

"I can't, Dona," I tried to say. "My strength is all squeezed out—"

The black mist was crowding upon me again. Now that the sharp pressure of agony was gone from throat and chest and limbs, a merciful darkness beckoned. Oblivion was a warm, soothing pool. It would heal all my injuries, cradle me forever.

"Bari—"

That soft familiar voice called to me urgently. It was a golden line that sought to draw me from the sea of soothing darkness, I clung to it. Dimly, I could once more see that white and lovely wraith floating above the shimmer of the diamond.

"Come, Bari!"

The phantom took my hand, drew my arm out of the silver loops.

"Your body is about to die, I know," she said. "But it has vital power enough for this last task. For the secret you gave me can aid us. Follow me!"

Her hand was suddenly cool and real in mine. She tugged again, and I stepped toward her, out of those metal coils—as easily as if they had turned to smoke.

I could see again! The dark-gleaming mirror beneath; the white robots sprawled upon it; the lax, twisted forms of Verel and Kel. I could see the woman beside me—the dark wealth of her red-glinting hair, the wide violet eyes of Dona and Dondara.

"We must hasten, Bari," she urged anxiously. "Or he will drop your body and the Stone into the mirror. Not even the power you gave me can reach him from outside the universe!"

We turned toward Malgarth, towering in the red gloom beyond that ebon film. His giant body swayed back in grotesque triumph, and the vast blue masses of his compound eyes were fixed upon something behind us.

Suddenly, queerly, as the hand of the woman tightened on mine, I was no longer Bary Horn. I was the Bari Horn legend had made me. All the knowledge that had gone into the building of Malgarth was a reservoir that I could tap.

Before me, strangely, just as I had seen it in that crystal-domed laboratory, was the brain of Malgarth. Black, vast, deeply convoluted, floating in a transparent tank. I saw the little pale spot upon its blackness. I knew the structural weakness in the synthetic brain, that I, Bari Horn, had been laboring to correct—and, at the urging of Dondara Keradin, had left uncorrected.

"Hurry!" she whispered beside me. "He believes that you are dead. He is reaching to drop us into the mirror!"

Fantastically, then, we were climbing into the mass of Malgarth. The body of the robot was a hundred-foot tower, crowded with all that compact mechanism that had made him master of the Galaxy. Passing through barriers of metal as if they had been but shadows, we came up at last to the robot's brain.

It has grown with the ages. Bathed in a huge, armored vat of purple liquid, fed by throbbing pumps, it was immense and black and deeply cleft. But still its shape was the same. And still there was that tiny, livid spot.

I reached for it—

But a queer shock deadened me. A dark film came between me and the brain. A curious inertia stopped my hand. I was sick with a sense of headlong, giddy falling. All the vast mechanisms of the robot's interior spun and grew dim about me.

Only the woman of the Stone remained real beside me, her hand electric on my own.

"Now!" she gasped. "He has flung us into the mirror!"

I fought that inertia. Desperately, I groped through that darkening film. Somehow, the black brain seemed to be spinning away from me, into infinity.

But I touched it. My fingers plunged deep into its wrinkled black mass, to that pale spot. I clutched, tore. The great brain quivered. It almost *writhed*. A blackness spread in the purple liquid.

"We're gone," sighed the woman. "His mirror—"

The brain, and the monstrous metal body, and all that incredible red-lit hall, were whirled away from us, as if upon a silent and resistless wind. There remained only the bright phantom, and myself, alone in a giddy void.

Very faintly, however, even in that featureless vertiginous gulf, the brazen voice of Malgarth reached me. Slow, bewildered, stricken, it was saying:

"My science lost! A thing so simple—and I did not know! A fluid-tube ruptured—the Stone knew—fear—

fear! They are cast into the mirror—Bari and the Stone— gone beyond returning. But I—who could have been eternal—*dying*—"

Even that failing voice was swept away. It was lost upon that mighty, soundless wind. And I knew that what seemed a wind was the supernal power of the geodesic mirror. It was the Stone and myself that it carried, not the things that we had left behind. And our destination must be some dark bourn beyond the limits of space. But a deep rejoining filled me, even in that spinning gulf. And the woman beside me said joyously:

"It is done, Bari. Our task of a million years is done. Malgarth is dead," her warm hand tightened on mine. And then it seemed to relax. I looked for her, in that starless chaos, and saw that once more she was growing dim, phantasmal. "Farewell, Bari," she whispered. "My heart, farewell!"

A terrible loneliness smote me.

"Dona, Dona, you can't leave me!" I cried into that vacant pit. "If you go, there will be—nothing! I'll be— *beyond*—alone!"

That beloved image was fainter than a wraith of mist. But the voice I loved came dimly, thinly, once again:

"I must go, Bari. I'm glad to go, after these weary ages of waiting. Even the Stone must die, Bari! And there is one mystery left. One veil that only death can pierce. I hope—I believe—that behind it we shall find what all our incarnations have strived for in vain."

I groped after her vanishing shadow.

"But, Dona!" I cried. "From where the mirror hurls us, there can be no returning. Malgarth said—"

"But Malgarth is dead!" the ghost of her voice came back. "He died before we were thrown outside the universe. Now his New Robots rule the mirror. And they are not evil, Bari, since his dominion is removed—things so beautiful could not be. They respect mankind, as the makers of the robots—and the destroyer of Malgarth! They promise now to be the friends of man, Bari—and the two races, striving in friendship together, can reach a greatness never dreamed of!

"They control the mirror, Bari. They can set its focus back in our universe."

"If they are friendly—" the question burned away my own concern "—what of the others? Verel and Kel? Is it too late—?"

"The science of the New Robots can save their lives," that receding voice told me. "They will be leaders among the survivors of mankind. They are weeping, now, for you, Bari."

"The other two?" I asked anxiously.

"Even they survive," said that dying whisper in the pit. "That same power of the mirror that hurled them out of space, the New Robots used to bring them back, before they perished. They cannot speak of what they saw beyond. The engineman is silently chewing his weed; the cook, sobbing for a drink."

The whisper faded. For a little time I was all alone in that strange lightless abysm. Frantically, I called the name of Dona, of Dondara, until the whisper came again:

"Farewell, Bari. I can see no more. Nor speak. For the Stone is dying. We must each go along through the mysterious portal ahead. I shall wait for you, beyond. Come to me, Bari!"

The thinning whisper was then lost forever in that crevasse of midnight. Whirling darkness pressed thick upon me, and cleared away. And I found that I was standing, reeling, in the middle of an unfamiliar room.

The walls cleared before my throbbing eyes. Gasping for breath, as if I had just that instant escaped the strangling tentacles of the robot, I staggered into a Morris chair. Wonderment overcame all my pain.

For the furnishings were those of my own age, my own country! There were familiar books on the shelves. The calendar above the writing desk was for October, 1938. The mirror of Malgarth, somehow, had set me back twelve hundred thousand years in time!

In my bruised hand, I suddenly discovered—in the same hand with which I had held the hand of that ghost of the Stone—was a great pellucid brick of diamond. The Stone itself!

Holding it up to the light, in trembling fingers, I could see deep within it a faint, tiny image—the lovely miniature of Dona, of Dondara Keradin. I called to it, desperately, but it did not move or answer. I tried even to warm life into the diamond, against my body. But the Stone was dead.

And my own body, it came to me as the first bitter fever of grief subsided, was also at the verge of death. Already weakened, doubtless, by the ages I had slept, it had now been crushed beyond recovery.

Working in some agony, I have been three days and nights writing this narrative. Strength for the task has come from what source I do not know. I want my son Barry to read it, and I am bequeathing to his care the jewel that was the Stone of Dondara.

I have made no appeal to medical aid. The questions of baffled medical science would have been too difficult for a dying man to answer. And I have no wish to live any longer. My work is done.

These long and painful days and nights have not been lonely. For the diamond lies beside me on the desk, and I have felt an unseen presence with me. It still seems strange for me, the scientist, the skeptic, to write that I yet hope to find the soul of her who was the Shadow of the Stone.

But I do.

THE END

A MONSTER FROM A PARALLEL WORLD

Over the air waves young Sally O'Neill's voice soared. It was a beautiful voice with all the qualities of a great singer, and it was bound to attract new listeners to the radio station. But then something happened— something that defied description. As her performance grew in intensity, the unique, piercing quality of her voice somehow caused a short circuit in the station's transmitter—in a split second they were thrown off the air! It appeared to be some kind of freak accident, but what no one could have guessed was that Sally O'Neill's voice had also ripped a hole in the barrier between Earth and an unknown parallel world. And during that brief moment, a strange robotic creature from that parallel world was hurtled into our universe. Unfortunately, the creature wanted to make sure the beautiful Miss O'Neill would never again cause such an accident…

CAST OF CHARACTERS

DAN MARSHALL

This radio engineer had big plans for his girlfriend's singing career. His only obstacle was an alien from another world!

SALLY O'NEILL

She had a good voice, a great voice. So great in fact that the sound of it could blow radio stations off the air.

YOLAN

It was an alien robot, and it was trapped on Earth when a freak occurrence at a radio station caused it to tumble into our world.

LETTIE LATOUR

She was a big time movie actress and nobody was going to tell her she hadn't seen a robot float into her bedroom boudoir.

RYKER

As talent agents went, he was one of the sleaziest around, but that never stopped him from shoving a contract into someone's face.

THE LINEMAN

There was thunder in the air the night he climbed a power pole out on Highway 18. He never realized just how close it was.

THE PILOT

His plane was struck by a strange force and he needed a landing place—quick. Failure to do so would cost his passengers' lives.

THE
FLOATING
ROBOT

By
DAVID WRIGHT O'BRIEN

ARMCHAIR FICTION
PO Box 4369, Medford, Oregon 97504

*For more information about Armchair Books and products, visit our
website at…*

www.armchairfiction.com

Or email us at…

armchairfiction@yahoo.com

CHAPTER ONE

THE name O'Neill and red hair and temper go naturally together, and Sally had 'em all. Right now Sally O'Neill was a red-headed fury on wheels, which was something because even when she wasn't mad, Sally was beautiful.

"Danny Marshall!" she literally flung both body and voice at the dazed young man standing before her, "how did this get out?"

"How did what get out?" asked Dan Marshall, devouring the flame of her with his eyes.

"This!" snapped Sally, thrusting an opened magazine under his nose.

"Oh, *Radio News*, hey," he blinked and drew his eyes into focus by the simple expedient of taking a backward step. Then they widened. "Honey, you mean we got some publicity—" He snatched the magazine from her.

"Publicity!" she screamed. "Oh, Dan Marshall, I could kill you—!"

He ignored her fury for the moment. " 'Small town girl blows fuse…' " he began reading, then stopped, swallowed hard, and crimsoned to his ears.

"How'd this get out?" he bellowed.

Sally's lips tightened. *"I'm* asking that question, Dan Marshall, and you'd better begin answering it."

Marshall's brow began to furrow in an annoyed frown and he gripped the magazine tighter as he read on. " 'Station KABL, Sharon Springs, Kansas, recently went off the air for over an hour on two separate occasions, when Miss

Sally O'Neill, soprano, kicked the daylights out of the power tubes with (you can take it or leave it) her high A over high C. It seems technician Daniel Marshall didn't account for the dynamite in this lovely (we hear) little lady's voice. Might we suggest a little back-pedaling on the volume rheostat next time, Danny?' "

There was a strained silence that grew more strained as his voice ceased.

"Well?" said Sally dangerously.

Marshall expelled his breath in a long whoosh, and looked at her. "I'm sorry, Sally," he said simply. "I don't know how the story got out. I didn't do it. And you know as well as I do, that our mutual contract to get you into the big-time means as much to me as it does to you. More, maybe, because after all, a guy wants the girl who's going to be his wife to get every break…"

"And I suppose you'll let the tubes blowout next Friday night when we go on the network," she told him. "Is that what you mean by 'breaks'?"

"Now, Sally…" he began pleadingly, "…how about giving me a break? After all, has an engineer ever had to contend with the kind of a voice you've got? I tell you, when you go out over the airwaves from coast to coast Friday night on the National Talent Roundup, you're going to hit Star Lane with a bang. And how can I put you over if I don't experiment first and make sure nothing will go wrong?"

"You've tried twice now," she pointed out. "It seems to me a little thing like turning a rheostat oughtn't be so hard."

HE tossed the magazine onto the desk and taking her slim shoulders in his hands, kissed her on the lips.

"Anything's hard, when it means taking my eyes off you," he grinned. "But seriously, honey, I'm sorry this all got out, and I'll promise that in the future that pesky little rheostat behaves. In fact, I'm putting you on the dinner concert this evening with the same number you'll sing Friday night—"

"Oh!" her eyes widened. "Your—aria!"

"—yeah—and make sure we have the volume under control," he finished with a rush. "That'll give us a chance to let you hit all those high notes in my composition, and—"

"But, Danny," she protested, "you weren't going to use it until Friday. You haven't even had it registered for copyright. Do you think you should?"

"Silly," he bantered. "Who's going to steal it? After all, you're the only one in the world, so far as I know, who can actually sing it, and anyway, without advance warning, who could get it down on paper?"

He backed away and looked her up and down critically. "Let's see," he mumbled, "you've never seen beauty until you've seen Sally. Hair the color of all the shades of red in a tropic sunset; eyes filled with the green of calm, deep water, but eyes that sometimes flash with the angry flame of a meteor from space; an ivory-white throat with a delicious indentation where the leaping pulse of fiery youth beats visibly; high, gleaming forehead; a form so exquisite that—"

"Danny Marshall," she interrupted abruptly, "are you drunk?"

He grinned at her impudently. "No. Just going over your good points for the publicity releases I'll be giving out after Friday…"

He halted as she turned and tripped lightly to a desk and a typewriter. Inserting a sheet of paper, she began typing. As she typed, she read aloud.

"Tall as a Greek god, and with wavy blond hair; eyes as blue as any seagoing Viking of old; a devil with the women; clumsy, especially when dealing with a rheostat; and oh so easy to forgive—"

The keys jammed as he leaned over the desk and kissed her again.

"Sally," he whispered, "you're a jewel…"

*   *   *

"WHAT a jewel," chuckled Martin Ryker, leaning back in his leather-cushioned desk chair, and shifting his big feet to a more comfortable position on the glass-topped desk of his New York office. "Small town girl blows tubes. That's rich. This writer Kinchell is a riot. Wonder where he gets all his gags?"

Martin Ryker read on. Suddenly his feet thudded to the floor and he sat up straight, his eyes widening.

"Saaay…" he muttered, the grin wiped from his face. "It takes a pretty steady jolt of juice to blow a main power tube. And it says here she's good looking. Maybe this ain't so funny after all…"

He jabbed a fat finger down on the buzzer button on his desk. Instantly a dapper secretary, whose ferret eyes belied any look of inoffensiveness his general appearance gave, came in.

Ryker threw the magazine at him. "Page 36," he barked. "Read the gag about the girl blowing the tubes at KABL. Then get out there by plane. Get a recording of her voice, and if it's any good, in your crooked opinion, slap a contract at her. Ham, grand opera, Chesterfield cigarettes, what's the difference. She's got power. This is the age of power. I don't miss any bets. And I got lots of contract blanks. Get going…"

Martin Ryker settled back in his seat, a thoughtful look on his face as the secretary scurried out. Then, after a moment, he grinned. "Rich," he chortled. "That guy Kinchell knows his onions. He's got a swell grapevine. Swell…"

*　　*　　*

"SHE'S swell, boss, swell! I got some of the sweetest glitter-stuff ever put in cans. And she ain't ham, boss. She's even too good for grand opera. She's good for a coffee program any day in the week.

"Where'm I callin' from? Right here in—what'sa name of this stinkin-little burg now?—oh yeah, Sharon Springs—

"Now wait a minute, boss, and let me finish tellin' yuh. That's why I'm calling from here. I didn't get no contract—yet. Y'see, it's a funny set-up, and I gotta work it out a little devious. It seems the gal is in love with the station director, this Dan Marshall guy, and they got it all stowed away in the Frigidaire. Yeah, he's gonna manage her, and get her on the top rung of the ladder of success, and then he's gonna marry her.

"Sure, boss, I talked to him. Not big money, you understand, because he's a smart boy and he has plans. I found out around town about him—plenty. The kind of a kid who has ideas of his own chain, and cleaning up on and in the big time. In fact, boss, he has been quoted as saying you're a stinking crook.

"No, boss, *I* didn't say that. Hold on, will you? Maybe you are, but *I* never say it. But he won't have nothing to do with us. And neither will she. His word is law with her, and he's the little tin god. She's plenty soft on him.

"Well, anyways, I didn't get to first base with offering her a contract. She says Danny boy is right smart, and he'll have her up there in no time.

"Sure you got time, boss. Here's the set-up. She goes on the air Friday night over the National Talent Round-up—

"Cripes, boss, I *know* it's a rival chain. But lemme finish. She ain't gonna make no hit over the Roundup. When she gets to that first high A over high C, the volume control won't cut down for her. Blooey! Get it? She blows another tube, and the local station goes off the air for a couple hours. Sally's sore at the boyfriend right now for the write-up Kinchell gave her. And if Danny-boy botches it up again, making her sound like an air raid warning just before the blackout, she's going to be hopping mad, and I wouldn't be surprised if she could be easily persuaded to tear up her contract with him, if she has one.

"But that ain't all. She sang a composition of the boyfriend's, written especially for that voice of hers, and it sure is a sweet one. The boy has talent. She's got the voice. Well, I found out he ain't had it copyrighted yet—in fact, it's still in the rough draft. The song, I mean. So I took the precaution to record the song as she sang it last night on the dinner concert.

"Yeah. I knew you'd know what to do in a case like this. That's why I rushed the wax recording to you this morning by airmail.

"You're coming down yourself to handle the girl? Okay with me. I'll see that the station goes off the air. That volume rheostat won't work at the proper time.

"Sure, boss, you can count on me for the dirty work…"

*   *   *

DAN MARSHALL glanced nervously at the minute hand of his watch, then fixed the control phones more firmly over his ears. It was time for Sally to go on the National Talent Roundup.

He caught the applause for the last section of the cross country pickup, and the announcer began his smooth, dramatically uttered introduction to the next section.

"…Miss Sally O'Neill, soprano!" he finished.

Marshall gave his meters a critical scrutiny, threw a switch that began a recording, then settled back to listen as the clear soprano voice of Sally O'Neill drifted into his ears. Her voice floated on, clear as a bell, tinkling in rising bars, ever higher.

Marshall leaned forward. "Now—" he whispered to himself.

Sally's voice soared upward, upward, then surged out in full volume. Marshall turned the rheostat down deftly. Suddenly his earphones began to blare, rattled deafeningly, then with an abrupt finality, went dead.

Marshall tore the phones from his head, his ears ringing. Then he became conscious that the ringing wasn't all in his ears. There was a high-pitched tone that still echoed through the locked control room, almost reverberating from the walls, as though some giant clock had just tolled the hour of one.

There was a sharp crackling sound, as of an electric arc sputtering somewhere. Then abruptly the lights dimmed. As though being muffled out by an invisible blanket of darkness, they faded away, to be replaced at last by intense blackness. Marshall sat paralyzed by the phenomenon, then he blinked. There was something before him in the darkness—something hanging in mid-air in that stygian gloom!

The hair prickled erect on his scalp and his spine crawled. For there, before his aching eyes, a glow came up; a brilliant crimson glow, shot with silver flashes of incandescence. And its light revealed the most fantastic being Marshall had ever seen in any nightmare.

It was a nameless thing of gleaming red metal, perhaps five feet in height. It had a formless head, with odd projections that might have been eyes, but there were no eyes in them. It had metallic arms, terminating in almost human hands. It had no legs, but a round bottom almost ludicrously like an untippable salt cellar, ringed by a band of what seemed to be radioactive gold.

And it floated effortlessly perhaps a foot above the floor.

Almost blinded by the angry flashings from its electrically alive body, Marshall shrank back in his chair.

"What is this...thing?" he gasped.

And then, to his utter horror, he felt his whole body possessed, his brain invaded, by a nameless vibration that somehow took the form of words. He was powerless to move, and listened in growing incredulity as a voice rang out soundlessly in his mind.

"I am Yolan... Is it you who have done this to me? Twice before you invaded my world in the ether; twice before you have tried to despoil me of my freedom. Now you have succeeded. I, understandably, condemn this. What is this horrible world into which you have called me? Why have you sought me out with your vibration that commands?"

Marshall was dazed and fought to regain his possession of his faculties. But he was helpless to answer. Instead, he felt his mind being probed, the answers being dug unmercifully from him. Replies that were meaningless, because not even he knew the answers.

He felt that the incredible thing before him was sifting out the things it drew from his brain; trying to catalogue them, understand them. And suddenly he knew that the thing was failing utterly.

"I am Yolan," repeated the monster, rather querulously. "What is this world? Why have I been trapped in this dark place? I am Yolan. I am Yolan."

Suddenly Marshall felt his brain released. He sensed in the doubting, shifting motions of the metal creature as it swayed in the air before him, that it was caught in the web of doubt, of indecision, of bewilderment perhaps even greater than his own.

Then the creature seemed to stiffen, become motionless, as though listening, or sensing something beyond Marshall's earthly perceptions.

There began a high pitched droning, a squeal that sounded oddly like the clashing heterodyning of an old-fashioned receiver. Then there came brilliant flashes of light, and a roar of awful sound.

Marshall sensed rather than saw that the creature was going to rush toward him, hurtle at him with metallic devastation.

Instinctively he threw himself prone, and for an instant, was bathed in an eerie electrical glow as the nameless bulk hurled over his prostrate form. Something struck his breast painfully. Then, with a terrific crash, a shower of plaster, wood, and bricks, it was gone. And in its place was a huge gap in the wall of the building through which a street light shone.

Down below, in the street, as Marshall picked himself dazedly up, a crowd was collecting.

"An explosion!" someone yelled. "The radio station has exploded!"

And then, inexplicably, the lights went on. Marshall stared around dazedly. They came on exactly as they had gone, as though a muffling blanket had been lifted from them.

On the stairway the thudding of feet came. Marshall staggered to the door and unlocked it, and a blue-coated policeman burst into view.

"Begorry," he gasped, "what's goin' on in here?"

"I don't know, Flanagan," said Marshall with tight lips. "Something...went past me, and burst through that wall as though it wasn't there. Something big, red, made of metal—and it floated in the air, with nothing to hold it up..."

Marshall stared appealingly at the frowning Flanagan.

"It was all lit up, like a weird ghost. It didn't have a face, and no legs. But it had arms, and hands, with long metal fingers—" Marshall indicated his shirt, which was torn over his breast. And underneath were bloody scratches that looked like the claw marks of a giant cat.

Flanagan frowned. He looked at Marshall. "Have you been drinking—" he began.

Dan Marshall shook his head. "No," he said hoarsely. "I saw it, Flanagan. And I'm sure I never want to see it again. Because there just can't be anything like that!"

Marshall staggered to the door and stepped out.

And stood face to face with a blazing-eyed, tight-lipped girl.

"DAN MARSHALL," she said, voice trembling, tiny fists clenching and unclenching stiffly at her sides. "An hour ago I would have drawn and quartered the man who called you a fool. But right now, I'd shake his hand. You, utter, complete, bungler. Do you know what you've done? You've made me the laughing stock of the country. Business manager! You couldn't manage to hold your breath long enough to embarrass the insurance company…"

Her eyes widened a moment as she saw the wreckage of the control room.

"My," she added acidly. "You've managed to blow up more than the tubes with my high notes, this time. The publicity on this will be simply wonderful. I'll be blowing up buildings and bridges next!"

"Sally," Marshall grabbed her arms. "Please… I didn't do all this. Some kind of strange metal robot did it. It came into the control room and spoke to me. It said its name was…Yolan. It hypnotized me, read my mind…" Abruptly Marshall stopped speaking, realizing how insane his hurried words were sounding. He saw the expression of utter disbelief and disgust that was sweeping over Sally's lovely features.

"Dan Marshall…" she said in utter amazed anger. "Dan Marshall—*you're drunk!*"

The cold fury in her tones rose in crescendo until she almost screamed. Suddenly with a furious motion, she wrenched her ring from her finger and threw it at him.

Then, sobbing, she whirled and ran from the studio into the night.

"Sally!" he called, sprinting after her, but at the door he stopped. There was no halting Sally now, he knew, and the sting where the ring had hit against his face made his heart sink to his shoes.

"Golly," he muttered. "She means that. Now I *am* in a jam."

Despondently he turned back to the studio and then halted as a dapper little man sauntered past, a slightly amazed expression apparent, even yet, on his rat-like face.

"What are you doing here?" asked Marshall in sudden suspicion.

"Nothing at all. For a time I still had hopes. But now—" The little man shrugged. "She had a nice voice," he said regretfully. "But I don't think anybody could do anything with it now. Unless you could use it for a factory whistle—"

"Why you little rat." Marshall said, clenching his fist.

The dapper little man ducked hurriedly past him into the night.

CHAPTER TWO
The Robot Runs Amok

"THERE just can't be anything like that, Miss Latour," the frantic, perspiring, red-faced Insurance Adjuster rasped despairingly. "We're willing to settle any reasonable claims. Especially when they involve a well-known movie actress like yourself. But when you tell us that some floating, red-metal thing-a-muh-bob comes into your, uh…ah…boudoir and shocks you into a faint—" He paused, almost hysterical, and mopped his brow. "Well, good heavens, Miss Latour, how can I tell my company that that's what they have to pay claim on?"

The raven-haired cinema star rose, pulling her dressing robe closer about her, eyes blazing.

"Do you mean to say that you think I'm lying?" she said with great intensity.

Her agent, a fat, bald little man with a thick accent rose quickly, putting his fat hand on her arm in an effort to calm her down. "Now, now, Lettie," he said quickly, "don't get excited."

She shook his hand from her arm, continuing to stare at the Insurance Adjuster. Her voice, as she spoke, was cold, low, and seething with indignation.

"For the last time," she said, "I'll tell you just what happened. And then your company better pay my claims, or I'll—"

"Please don't get too up in arms about this, Lettie," her Agent implored.

"Shut up!" the actress shouted. "This *thing* came into my room! I was telephoning long distance, New York. The operator had given us the connection, and I'd talked for almost two minutes when the hook-in seemed to grow fainter. Then there was a confusion of static. The phone began to crackle like…like…something alive. Then this horrible thing came floating into the room!"

The very recollection of the incident seemed to flood her with horror, for she pulled her dressing robe closer, shuddering, face pale.

"If you don't settle for my emotional shock and distress, and settle plenty—" she repeated ominously. Her voice rose shrilly. "It was terrible, I tell you, terrible!"

The Insurance Adjuster was at the door. "Okay, Miss Latour. I swear I'll do all I can. We settle. But don't let this thing get into the newspapers. If some of the other hams—uh, actresses, around Hollywood got wind that our company was paying for claims like that…" He paused to shudder. "…it would break us."

When the Adjuster was gone, the Agent turned to the actress. He rubbed his chubby paws, beaming.

"Wonderful, Lettie, colossal! What a news story…what publicity, little girl! How did you ever think of it? A metal monster visits film cutie. Now I can just see the headlines…"

The actress was gazing stonily at the little Agent, her eyes once more kindling sparks. "You imbecile," she grated. "There *was* such a monster. I tell you I saw it!"

The Agent's face whitened. He backed toward the door. "But Lettie," he said. "There just *can't* be anything like that."

He slipped out of the door just in time to avoid a flying paper weight.

*   *   *

IT was after midnight as the rotund, middle-aged radio "ham" closed the door behind him in his attic and, with the dazed and loving expression of an addict, walked over to his apparatus in the corner of his room. His gait was a trifle unsteady, for the party he had just returned from had been quite generously flooded with Cheering Nectar,

But a "ham" being a "ham"—drunk or sober—he was sitting at his set five minutes later, earphones on his head, intoning blearily into the small mike before him.

"C-Q, calling C-Q," the mellow and middle-aged gentleman said.

"Hello, C-Q, hello C-Q," he repeated.

For a while he sat there, waiting for response. Then, slightly annoyed, he made an adjustment on the control board in front of him. Static seemed to be bad tonight, terrible.

"Hello C-Q," the inebriated gentleman mumbled. "Damn, hello C-Q!"

Suddenly he sat bolt upright, an expression of extreme confusion wreathing his face. He made another adjustment, then another. In the silence of the room, the crackling response in his earphones seemed unnecessarily loud. A third adjustment, and the crackling became still louder.

The tubes on the control apparatus were glowing redly, more and more brilliantly. The "ham" tried to rise from his seat, tried to get the earphones off of his head. He failed in both attempts, and sat there, mouth agape, while the control board itself began to crackle.

There was a terrific explosion, followed by a series of wild, lightning-like flashes! The entire attic seemed bathed in a brilliant, static light. The "ham" had been thrown from his seat by the concussion, the earphones jarred from his head!

A crash of glass—and the attic window was shattered. Something red, something metal, glowing, weaving, floated into the room...

The "ham" tried to scream, tried to shout. The din and the flashing continued. Blackness closed around him.

PRECISELY TEN minutes later, his wife was helping him to his feet. She was little, gray-haired, and angry. The confusion in the room was silenced. The attic was once more peaceful. But the window was broken, and his radio apparatus was a charred, twisted thing in the corner.

"You'll have to make up your mind," his wife was saying. "Either confine yourself to radio as a hobby, or drinking. But you can't mix them both. I knew something like this would happen sooner or later."

Sobered and shaken, the "ham" stood there, looking doubtfully around the attic. He opened his mouth and was going to tell his wife about the floating thing, the red metal thing. Then he clamped his jaws shut. Hell. It hadn't happened. There just couldn't be anything like that...

FROM THE MORNING EDITION of the *Newhaven Times:*

Last night the entire community was thrown into utter darkness when a breakdown occurred at the city power plant. For twenty hours Newhaven was without electric lights or electric power.

In a sworn statement, the night shift at the power plant declared that the breakdown was caused by forces beyond their control—that some tremendous electrical force, a floating, inhuman thing, invaded the plant, blowing out the turbines completely.

FROM THE EVENING EDITION of the *Chicago Record-Herald:*

AIRLINER CRASHES, TWELVE DIE
SENATOR NORDERHOFF KILLED

(USP) The mysterious crash of the gigantic, Chicago-bound Midwestern Airliner, in the Michigan Dunes early this morning has already had nationwide results in its implications. An immediate investigation by the Interstate Air Commission has been demanded by local authorities who investigated the scene of the crash.

The disaster, which resulted in the death of Senator James L. Norderhoff (Dem. Ia.), and eleven others, occurred at approximately five-thirty this morning.

Co-pilot, Jess Weems, is still lingering between life and death at the State Hospital.

The condition of the plane, which didn't burn when it crashed, leads authorities to suspect that the cause of the crash might have been something other than a mechanical one. The motor was still in almost perfect condition upon inspection. The rear of the fuselage, however, was practically torn away.

Co-pilot Weems, although delirious, has made several strange statements which led authorities to believe that some human agency engineered the accident. These statements indicate that someone, perhaps one of the passengers forced a way into the pilot's compartment to deliberately wreck the ship, which was following a radio beam into Chicago.

EXCERPT FROM NEWS STORY in the *Miami Times:*

CRUISE LINER ON REEF
RADIO BEAM BLAMED

A strange radio static condition, which last night held the Key West area in a state of electrical confusion, was blamed for the miscalculations made through radio beam by the officers of the cruise liner *Floridan,* and is said to have resulted in the reef shoaling of the vessel.

Passengers aboard the *Floridan* gave strangely conflicting opinions as to the cause of the grounding. Some of them attested that they could see weird lightning flashes that occasionally pierced the fog. Others, undoubtedly influenced by the well-known Loch Ness Sea Monster myth, swear to having seen an odd, red, glowing creature floating in and out between the electrical storm bursts. These statements however, have been discounted by Captain Rolf Peterson.

*   *   *

THE telephone lineman climbed out of the truck, pausing to strap his pole-climbing apparatus on his legs. The broad, straight stretch of Highway Eighteen was like a shimmering ribbon of mirror as the fine mist of rain sprayed relentlessly down from the darkened skies.

The lineman turned to his partner, a stocky barrel-chested little fellow wearing a black cap pulled low over his eyes. The lineman was tall, and he had to bend over to shout into the little man's ear, for it was difficult to be heard above the rumbling thunder overhead.

"This is a helluva night, Shorty," the Lineman bellowed. "I wish I was home and in bed."

Shorty grinned and pulled his cap lower over his eyes, fishing for a crumpled pack of cigarettes in his pocket. "Don't worry me none," he shouted in response. "You gotta do the climbing..."

The Lineman grinned, then, and Shorty went to the back of the truck to get his apparatus. When he returned, the Lineman was standing beside the tall telephone pole some four yards off the edge of the highway.

"Hurry up," the Lineman shouted. "Wanta get up and get done with it. Then we can catch some java and sinkers down the road."

Shorty nodded, handing him his equipment, then stepped back, watching as the Lineman began his ascent of the pole. The Lineman's spikes dug deep in the wood, and in a few moments he neared the top. From his perch, he could look down on the stocky, small figure of his helper. The rain was heavier, now, beating into the Lineman's face.

The thunder rolled louder, ominously, and then was followed by a smashing detonation. The pole seemed to sway. The Lineman looked down the road, along the tops of the other poles, squinting through the rain. Then his eyes widened incredulously.

Far down the line, perhaps a mile and a half away, he saw a rapidly growing orange-and-red ball of flame!

He watched, fascinated. The thing crackled along the telephone lines, flashes of electrical sparks shooting off in its wake. He opened his mouth; then snapped it shut. The pole was literally trembling from some strange vibration.

The wires next to his elbow were buzzing, and he felt the heat of them even through his thick jacket. Frantically, he moved back, his spikes digging into wood. There was one thought, now that he'd been galvanized into action— get down!

From the ground, he heard a shout, hoarse, terrified; Shorty's voice. Then, looking up again, he screamed wildly. The terrifically rushing ball of crackling sparks and orange flame was less than forty yards from him, moving with incredible speed!

But he was too late. The thing was upon him!

Blazing, crashing, numbing flashes seared his mind and stunned his body. He felt himself falling, falling—

SHORTY MET the nurse outside the door of the Lineman's hospital ward room.

"How is he?" he asked shakily.

"He'll be all right," she answered. And Shorty knew from the tone of her voice that she meant it. "You won't be able to see him until tomorrow," she concluded.

Shorty turned away. Electrical shock was what he'd told them. But God, that thing hadn't been an electrical shock! It was...it was...Shorty shuddered, seeking a word. There just couldn't be anything like it!

CHAPTER THREE
Key to a Monster

DAN MARSHALL snapped on the radio in his hotel room, adjusted the volume rheostat and then listened intently as the voice of the announcer suddenly swelled into being.

"Attention ladies and gentlemen! A special late bulletin from Florida. During an electrical storm in that region, witnesses reported the appearance of a strange comet-like object that appeared suddenly and flashed away out of sight before its exact nature could be ascertained. The witnesses state further that numerous bolts of lightning struck the object as if attracted to it by some strange magnetic force. The city officials are checking into the matter. Keep tuned to this—"

Dan Marshall cut off the voice with a vicious twist of his wrist and ran an impatient hand through his rumpled hair.

"That's the fourth report today," he muttered to himself. "What the hell's back of these electrical disturbances? Power plants, radio stations, wireless units, all turned upside down. And with every one of these freakish disturbances the witnesses have mentioned a floating, flaming object, or something like that. It can't just be a coincidence."

He paced the floor of his room nervously. At the back of his brain an insistent fear was plucking. What was the thing that had accosted him, then blasted out of the radio station?

He frowned thoughtfully. Was the thing that had been "born," so to speak, at the radio station, the same thing that was responsible for the freakish occurrences throughout the country?

As wild as that might sound it was as logical a guess as any other until someone unearthed more definite facts about the queer creature of the ether.

What kind of a thing was it? What furnished its energy; the terrible blasting energy that could shatter without effort a wall of concrete and steel? Did it have any directional intelligence or was it just a physical projection of strange radio waves?

These questions, Marshall knew, would have to be answered before anyone could do any more than guess about the weird being.

And in the meantime he had problems of his own and his main problem concerned a green eyed bundle of feminine dynamite—Sally O'Neill!

Furious over the blow-out at the station, she was ready to sign a contract with the man, Ryker, who had flown in. She had agreed to fly to New York with him for an audition.

Marshall pounded his big fist into the palm of his hand viciously. He was convinced the grinning, smirking fellow was rotten to the core. He didn't give a hang about himself but he didn't want Sally to be taken for a ride.

He had just made up his mind to make another attempt to change Sally's mind when there came a knock on the door. He crossed to it, opened it. Sally was standing there. Under her arm was a bundle of newspapers.

"May I come in?" she asked, in a tone of voice that would have bored through chrome steel.

MARSHALL knew the storm signals. The flashing green eyes, the gorgeous mass of red hair tossed back that way from her proudly held head spelled trouble. He grinned and stepped aside.

"Welcome, your gracious Majesty," he bowed low as she swept past him. "This humble domain is yours forever and I am yours to command."

He forced a mask of impassive gravity over his face and took her by the arm and led her to an overstuffed chair.

"The throne is just a bit dusty but ever since we went off the Gold Standard we can't afford maid service. However..." He turned her around, put both hands on her shoulders and pushed her gently into the chair. "...if it were brocaded satin on solid gold it would still be unworthy—"

"Dan Marshall," she interrupted ominously, "will you stop that nonsense and listen to me?"

He looked at her closely. "You sound very grim, my dear. Outside sparrows are twittering—"

"They're not sparrows," she corrected him automatically. "They're robins."

"Robins they are, then," he agreed, "but anyway they're twittering happily, the sun is shining, God's in his heaven, everything's cheerful and bright—and look at you. You should be laughing, smiling—"

"Smiling!" she cried. "What have I got to smile about? I've got nothing to laugh at. But thanks to you the whole country is laughing at *me*. Have you seen the morning papers?" she demanded suddenly.

"Well, as a matter of fact," he admitted, "I haven't. But..." He peered at the bundle of papers in her arm. "...I have a very definite feeling that I'm going to before I'm much older."

"You're right for once," she snapped. She thrust the papers at him. "Read them. You'll get a big kick out of them. They're positively hilarious. All about the—the—vocal freak. I believe that's the expression one brilliant reporter coined."

Marshall shuffled rapidly through the papers, turning to the entertainment columns and glancing at the articles relating to the broadcast of the night before. He read a few chapters from each story and winced.

They hadn't pulled any punches. All of the papers had gone to town on the story, treating Sally as if she were some fantastic freak, who shouldn't be allowed on the air waves. But some of the stories, Marshall was forced to admit were really funny. For instance the radio critic of the *Memphis Gazette* had written:

"It is our opinion that Miss O'Neill's peculiar vocal qualities would be admirably suited to the *Lights Out* program. Think of it! The announcer would introduce the program with—Light's Out! Miss O'Neill would hit her high note—and then they *would* be!"

Marshall chuckled. An instant later he realized what a mistake that was.

"Oh," Sally's voice was outraged, "so you think it's funny too!" She sprang to her feet and looked eagerly about for something to throw. Fortunately for Dan Marshall there wasn't anything movable within reach. With a helpless moan she sank back into the chair.

"THAT'S the last straw," she said bitterly. "After getting me into this trouble, making me the laughing stock of the country, ruining my chances of a radio career, you still have the nerve to think there's something funny about it."

"Now wait a minute, honey," Marshall sank to his knees beside her and tried to capture one of her hands, but she kept them firmly locked in her lap. "I didn't mean to laugh. You've gotta believe me when I tell you that I feel worse than you do about the whole thing. I feel like thirty-three varieties of rat and I'm not just being dramatic. I wanted you to go over. That's all I've been working for, dreaming of, for all these years. Together with my aria and your voice I didn't think anything could ever stop us. And nothing will. This mechanical trouble we can straighten out and then we'll be on our way up."

"All this has a familiar ring to it," Sally commented frostily.

"I know it," Marshall snapped. "I've said it over and over again because I mean it. Another thing: I don't believe your voice threw us off the air the last time. I think that rheostat was tampered with in some way."

Marshall snapped his fingers excitedly. What a stupid blundering fool he was. Why hadn't he thought of that before?

"Of course," he cried excitedly, "that's it."

He thought swiftly, the whole jumbled assortments of fact falling into a clear picture in his mind. Ryker wanted Sally's contract. What more logical than to make Sally look bad, make her look like a useless vocal freak, then make her an offer. Sure that she was something Sally would snap at as a last hope. Which was just what she had done. That's what Ryker's agent had been doing near the control room. He'd tampered with the mechanism so that it wouldn't respond to the rheostat.

"Don't you see, honey," he spoke swiftly, excitedly. "Ryker wanted you to think you were no good so he contrived to mess up the broadcast. Don't you see by signing a contract and going to New York with him you're playing right into his hands?"

"You haven't any proof of that," Sally challenged doubtfully, "and I don't think you *could* prove it. Mr. Ryker is taking me now when no one else wants me. He is willing to take a chance on my voice and give me a break. That's more than the other networks would do."

"Who said nobody wants you?" Marshall snapped belligerently. "You're going to be the hottest thing in radio and nothing's going to stop you. You've got the most glorious set of pipes that the ether has ever heard and you're feeling grateful because some two-bit chiseler like Ryker is going to audition you, because some big combine is trying to buy up talent at about one-tenth of what it's worth."

"Combine?" she snapped. "That sounds very encouraging to me. At least they'll have money. They'll be able to provide decent equipment that won't get temperamental every time someone turns on a little extra volume. It won't be a small, half-dozen watt station that spends as much time off the air as it does on. At least they'll be able to give me the opportunity of singing without fear of blowing up the control room!

"That's all I want. An opportunity to be heard. They'll give me that, and I'll be able to stand or fall on the merits of my voice alone. I'll be able to concentrate on my vocal production without worrying about inefficient engineers, cheap equipment, shortage of power—and you, Dan Marshall…"

She tossed her head defiantly.

MARSHALL put his hands on his hips and stared down at her. For a moment he said nothing, then he whistled softly.

"If I hadn't heard it," he said quietly, "I wouldn't have believed it."

Sally twisted uncomfortably under his gaze and averted her eyes.

"Well," she said, after a painful silence, "I have to think of myself don't I? I have to take advantage of an opportunity that will give me the things I want."

She looked up anxiously at his silent figure. "Well," she cried defensively, "don't I?"

Marshall's features were strained and white. "Sure," he said wearily, "you've got to look out for yourself, baby, and I don't think there's any question about your being able to do it. We're small time down here and you belong in the big time. The boys down here have helped you a bit but that's all right. Don't worry about *that!* You're going up. You've got the right technique. Don't take along any excess baggage. Use people, sure that's okay, but when they become a nuisance just dust 'em off like a fly speck."

He turned without glancing at her and crossed the room to the window. Without looking back he said, "Good luck, Sally."

Sally looked at his stiff, proud back and suddenly she was out of the chair, running to him, sobbing.

"Oh Dan, I didn't mean it," she cried. "I didn't mean it. I couldn't leave you, you know that. It was hateful of me to say the things I did."

He turned to her, his face lighting suddenly, and she buried hers against his chest. "I was angry, foolish, Dan, please forgive me," she murmured against his shoulder. "I'm not going to New York. We'll go together or not at all. I'll tell them to—to jump in the lake. There'll be other chances and we'll take them together. I don't care about anything except being with you. Everything's all right again, isn't it, Dan? Please say everything's all right again."

DAN MARSHALL didn't answer. Instead he did some fast thinking. He was realizing, perhaps for the first time in his life, how much Sally meant to him, and he was also realizing that he was standing in the way of her career. There was no doubt of it. What she said in the heat of anger and wounded pride had been the bitter truth. Sally needed good equipment to handle her glorious voice, expert publicity men, all the things that the others could give her and he could not. Her loyalty to him prevented her from accepting another offer, the offer that would lead her to stardom and fame. If she stuck with him she might never get there. He couldn't allow her to sacrifice herself for him. He had to make her take that offer, go to New York and there was only one way that he could do that. He hated to do it, but it was the only way he could drive her away from him.

"Stop sniveling," he snapped. "That won't make any impression on me."

She stepped back from him and dabbed at her eyes with her handkerchief.

"I'm sorry," she said, "but please don't be angry, Dan. I forgot myself for a minute because I was so disappointed and hurt that I wanted to hurt someone else. Please forgive me."

"Bravo, bravo," he jeered, "very good acting my dear. You really should be in Hollywood. Radio neglects your histrionic ability completely. But in spite of your cleverness it's no go. I'm sorry to disappoint you, but I'm not as simple as I look."

"Dan," she cried sharply, "what do you mean?"

"Aha," he smiled, "more acting. As if you didn't know. But if you really want me to draw a diagram I shall. Although I feel it's really unnecessary. In the first place you know that you're going to have a hell of a job cracking the eastern networks. Your voice isn't the greatest in the world, y'know, and on top of that you're liable to knock the station off the air before you get through. Knowing all this you realize that your chances are slim indeed unless you can get something different and sensational and inspiring to sing."

"Oh, Dan," Sally cried, "that's—"

"Let me finish," Marshall tried to keep his voice hard and brittle. "You knew this and you knew that if you could twist me around your finger I'd let you take my aria to New York with you. Well it was a good try, but it didn't work. You go to New York—without the aria. You were always just an investment to me and you turned out to be a darned poor investment. Why I even pretended to be nuts about you." He turned abruptly at the sight of her face and stared unseeingly out the window.

"Yeah, I—I even was that silly. Just to get you to put a little more oomph into your singing, but even that didn't help. Any way you look at it, you were a complete bust to me. But I draw the line when you try to steal my aria!"

Sally backed away a step, her hand crawling to her throat. "No—no Dan," she said weakly, "you don't mean it. You're joking. Please say you're just joking."

Marshall felt something like a cold hand closing over his heart, but he forced his voice to carry a note of nonchalant derision.

"The answer is still no, baby. Get it through that pretty head of yours that I mean it. You're a smooth article, but you're just not smooth enough. I've got work to do so I'll have to ask you to stop annoying Uncle Danny. Drop me a line when you hit the city, kid."

Marshall waited for an instant and then looked over his shoulder. The door to the corridor was open and the room was empty. Sally had gone.

MARSHALL sank into a chair and buried his head in his arms. For a long time he remained motionless and when he raised his head, his face was white and haggard with suffering.

"I did it," he muttered to himself. "I'd rather have stuck my hand into a furnace than hurt that kid, but it's for her own good. Someday she'll thank me."

So Dan Marshall sat there numbly, the anguish at what he'd been forced to do driving all other thoughts from his mind. Sally, gone this time for good. But it was better. It had to be better this way. Quick, and final.

Hours passed, while Marshall remained there in his room, quite alone with his grief. But the nostalgic recollections of Sally were becoming more than he could bear. Enough was enough. At last he rose, conscious that he must do something, anything, to drive this hellish torture from his mind.

Now he felt a sudden burst of rage, a futile, maddening sort of rage, at the thing that had been responsible for this.

Dan Marshall tightened his fists as a vivid light flashed in his brain. There was a way—

Crossing to his bureau drawer, he fished into a pile of odds and ends, bringing forth a stub nosed automatic pistol. It might be handy, for a plan that was already forming in his mind; a plan that had to do with a certain recording.

Marshall strode out of his room. Twenty minutes later, in the growing darkness, he was at the radio station.

LOCKING the doors, he went to the control room. There he secured the recording of that fatal Friday night Talent broadcast. The record that had been impressing in its waxen self the clear tones of Sally's voice, singing his aria.

Marshall had a theory concerning that record, that voice, that aria. A theory that tied in now, with growing clarity in his mind, with the weird red metal menace that had first appeared in this very same control room.

As he thought of the incident, Marshall stared at the temporarily closed wall of the room; the one that had been wrecked by the impetuous and powerful plunge of the metal horror toward some unknown destination.

It had been through that wall that the monster had gone, to create all the havoc the newspapers had been bewilderedly telling of in the past twenty-four hours. Through the radio that thing had come, and through radio and electrical waves it seemed to travel. Take, for instance, the case of the ship wrecked because its radio beam signals were awry. Or the telephone lineman who had been so weirdly jolted from his perch atop a power pole. Or the powerhouse that had gone dead in the middle of the night, completely wrecked by a weird red phantom creature that literally sucked the energy from whirling dynamos, and shorted expensive machinery. Or the crash of the air liner, causing the death of Senator Norderhoff.

Marshall thought he knew the answer now. The strange radio waves generated by Sally's unusual voice had been the real key to the red menace. Those waves had brought it blindly into being in this very room, torn from a strange world of its own, perhaps even in another dimension. It had accused him of exactly that. But then Marshall hadn't understood.

Then, bewildered by its presence in an utterly strange place, it had sensed something, gone plunging to seek it. Had that something been the radio beam that guided the Senator's plane? Had the uncanny robot flung itself along that beam, seeking a way to return to the world it called its own, and thus crashed blindly, with the same force it had used to smash through the wall, into the plane, sending it hurtling in flames to the Michigan Sand Dunes?

The implications were stunning to Marshall, and now, with the record that he instinctively felt held the key to the floating demon in his hand, he felt his rage subside; the rage that had made him want to do something dangerous, anything, just so he could forget Sally. Did he really want to broadcast Sally's voice once again, using the record, and recall that flaming horror to this station?

Marshall grinned, suddenly, recklessly. What the hell. What did he care what happened? He'd faced the thing before—talked with it. He'd do it again, and maybe this time send it back to the place it sought; the place from which it came. He'd talk to it again. He knew it had intelligence. It would understand now, what he could tell it. He would send it back forever to its own world. He would prevent the tragedies that were taking place, perhaps more of them even now, as the robot-creature plunged madly about the country, seeking a way out of its strange dilemma.

He made his way purposefully to the broadcast room. If his hunch was right, the flaming, floating robot would be forced to return to the studio when he played those key notes that obviously impelled the creature irresistibly to their source.

IN a matter of fifteen minutes he was ready. Then, his hand on the switch that would put Station KABL on the air, he stopped, his face a mask of chagrin. But he grinned shortly after a moment. This was going to be expensive, because when he played that record, it meant more blown-out tubes.

Abruptly he pulled the switch down, then started the recording. Hastily he barked the required announcement and call-letters into the ether, then stepped across the room, back against the wall, waiting tensely. He could hear nothing, except the faint scratching of the needle on the recording. He hadn't turned on the speaker. A moment, then suddenly the meters on the control panel leaped, flickered back and forth, then slammed back against the zero-post with finality.

"There she goes!" said Marshall grimly, aloud.

And with the words, there came the now familiar shrill heterodyning noise, the crackle of a vast kind of static, and brilliant flashes of red and white light. And abruptly, there in the deserted radio station, blackness descended, like a mantle, and the lights blanked out. For a moment Marshall stood in darkness lit by alternately flaming bursts of red and white. Then a brilliant crimson glare filled the room, making it seem like a scene out of Dante's Inferno and there, in the center of the room, floating motionless, except for a slight bewildered swaying was—the Radio Robot!

Marshall stood stiffly, hardly aware that in the tenseness of the moment he had drawn his automatic and held it leveled in his hand. His breath seemed frozen in his lungs, and his hair prickled on his scalp. This time, unlike the first appearance of the terror, he could see all the details of it plainly. And an unnamed, unreasoning fear gripped him. This was nothing earthly. It was nothing remotely human. It was—alien! Utterly and impossibly alien.

The robot floated quietly a moment, seeming to regard him with its eyeless eyes. Marshall felt some queer, unhuman sense observing him, groping to understand him. And he waited.

But then, abruptly, realization of danger flooded over him. He felt invisible fingers plucking at his brain, felt his body begin to go numb under the devilish spell of the monster. Once again, as it had that first time, the creature was taking possession of his body and his will. But not completely, yet. Marshall knew that he could still command himself to a limited extent, could still force his body to obey, although sluggishly, under tremendous mental effort, the commands of his enmeshed will.

He tightened his fingers about the butt of the gun.

CHAPTER FOUR
Secret of the Robot

THE automatic was kicking against his rigid grip and blasting deafeningly in the silence of the room, while vivid flashes shot through the crimson darkness. But the horrible vision remained swaying there before him, even though he triggered again and again.

A last empty click told Marshall that his ammunition was exhausted. And he stood there, frozen, while the stench of gun smoke burned his nostrils and the room rang from the shots. His useless weapon slipped from nerveless fingers, and even as it did—*the thing talked!* Calmly, coldly, as though his shots had gone unnoticed.

There were no sounds, but there was a voice. There was no language—but words stamped themselves on his mind! And dazedly, horrified, Marshall watched the creature floating redly before his eyes, while thought communications burned into his brain.

"It is no good. You are not able to harm me. I, Yolan, am not of your world. The weapons of your world are useless against me. I seek a way back. I have been hurled into your sphere through no wishes of mine. I seek a way back. I am Yolan. I come from—"

And as the words broke off, Marshall had another form of impressions registered upon him, weird, odd, eerie mental photographic visions. Familiar vision—like newsreels of incredible numbers jumbled on a gigantic screen; of songs, music, speeches, dramas; of garbled commercial announcements. An utterly fantastic montage of half-human things, of unhuman things.

And somehow, too, Marshall got the impression of this world in relation to his own—another dimension was its border, another plane of existence marked the span that divided it from his own. But it had the same sun, the same moon, the same stars and stratosphere. And then the visions blurred, the montage fading out of focus until it was but a gray blot.

The words resumed, once again hammering against Marshall's consciousness. "That is my world. The world from which I was taken. The world to which I seek return. I am Yolan. It was here that I was snapped into your world through some strange gateway. It is here that the gateway must still exist. I seek that door back from your world to mine. I must return. I am Yolan."

Somehow, Marshall was speaking. He hadn't been conscious of anything but the incredible apparition, its fantastic powers. But now the words were tumbling from his lips and he was powerless to stop them. It was once more as though he were being drained of all his thoughts, as though the robot were forcing him, in some strange manner, to speak.

And even as he talked, Marshall was aware that the words he spoke were the results of the conscious thoughts in his mind. He heard himself, as if from a distance, narrating a wild mixture of fear, anxiety, rage and all the emotions he had felt upon his entrance to the studio, in addition to a recounting of the panoramic emotions that had registered upon him when the radio robot had first appeared.

The odd monstrosity seemed to be digesting all this, sorting it. But, too, Marshall realized that while this was going on he had insight into the thought processes of the creature. Evidently the radio robot was forced to leave it-self vulnerable when seeking radio-mental information from others. Like an open connection on either end of an actual radio wave transmission—both able to send and receive communications.

STRANGELY, Marshall's sensations of fear had left him. His wonder and astonishment remained, but his mind had regained its ability to estimate the situation coolly. The danger, obviously, remained. But Marshall was now oblivious to it. And now his voice had ceased.

The creature still swayed before him, the heterodyning shrilling audible once more. The glow to its body was strong enough to produce illumination in the room, strong enough to bring into sharp relief the trailing arms and metallic fingered hands of it.

Slowly, Marshall could feel its mind processes digesting the information that it had sucked from his conscious thoughts. Methodically, the thing was sorting, and as it arrived at conclusions, those same conclusions were instantly apparent to Marshall.

The robot was recognizing, dimly, the reasons for Marshall's visit to the studio. Then this information was pushed aside, as the creature groped onward toward what it was seeking—information by which it could find its way out of this strange world into which it had been thrust; groping, determinedly toward that solution. Dan Marshall could feel the robot's brain searching for that information.

It was evident that the creature had at first suspected Marshall was among those responsible for its transmigration from its own world into this. But now, as the thoughts it had sucked from Marshall's brain failed to lead it to the pattern it sought, the thing seemed to be filled with a frantic bewilderment. An instant later thought-words stamped themselves on Marshall's mind once more. The robot-like creature was again speaking to him.

"It was here that the door existed. You must know of the door."

And at the question, panic once more struck into Marshall's heart. Too late he realized the situation. The gateway! The robot wanted to know the gateway. And that gateway was—Sally!

Instantly Marshall knew he must keep the secret from the robot. The evil that he sensed in the creature's disregard, or was it lack of knowledge, of living things of this strange world, would be vented upon her helpless head, if the robot discovered she was his only hope of returning to his own world. And Marshall knew now that this was true. Sally O'Neill, singing his aria, with her once-in-a-thousand-years voice, was the key to the door to the other world, just as the high note was the summoning command that tore him from it. If the robot discovered what it was that had brought him, he would seek the means to reverse the action. He would seek out Sally, and try to use her to return to his own weird domain of ether waves.

He, Dan Marshall, must lie successfully to a creature that could command his mind, overpower his will by sheer overbearing intelligence and mental force. As though from a distance he heard his voice saying: "I don't. I know nothing of how you came here."

"There was a door," the creature insisted, "through which I was brought here. A door that must still be here. I, Yolan, must find that door. I must return." Suddenly he seemed to glow more redly, and jerked right and left as though blown by sharp gusts. Marshall had a sudden

172

sensation that the creature's reactions were turning from bewilderment to frustrated rage.

And then Dan Marshall knew—realized he was being driven, against his will, to think logically toward the solution the robot sought, to seek some explanation of how this had come about, how this strange creature had been hurled from his own dimension into this! And he was unable to prevent himself from answering.

"RADIO," Dan was saying unable to stop the words that tumbled from his unwilling lips. "You're from a world of another dimension, a world living side by side with ours, an other-dimensional radio world. Your entrance into our world occurred at a radio station, this station. Your entrance from the radio world must have come through radio." As Marshall spoke these halting, elementary sentences, he realized that the radio robot was using his mind, blindly probing his knowledge of the natural world, to gain information which the robot itself was unable to comprehend!

"You entered our world through this station," Marshall continued, "at a time when—" and then Marshall tried to halt the words he knew were coming.

But his struggle was short-lived. His mind, battling desperately against the will forces of the robot, seemed to bend back in against itself until he could stand it no longer. Marshall gave in—and the words tumbled from his lips.

"At a time when," Marshall continued, "Sally had just blown the station hook-up with the high note she took. The high note that wasn't controlled by the engineer." And suddenly Marshall's voice stopped. It was as though the force which had been impelling him had unexpectedly ceased—because the robot had gotten its desired information.

There was an ominous silence in the darkness of the room. A silence in which the weird, suspended monstrosity glowed strangely, while Marshall felt the creature digesting the information.

"I understand. It is clear to Yolan now," the robot's words again burned into Marshall's brain. "It is this Sally creature. She holds the key to the door. The power by which I was torn from my world."

Marshall felt his scalp tingling at the menace of the words, cursing himself wildly for not having had the strength to resist the will of the radio robot. Sally—he'd betrayed her. This monstrosity would—Marshall choked off the thought. He had to get away, quickly, before he was again drained of more information by the monstrous floating thing!

He tried to turn, but he seemed to be literally frozen, unable to move his legs or twist his body. Then the voice of the radio creature was sending words to his brain once more.

"This Sally creature. I must find her. I know now, given time, how to open the door and return to my own world. But it will do me no good to return, if she lives. For she has the key—the power, to call me, against my will, back here. That must not happen again after I return. So I must kill her. You shall tell me where to find her. You must! You will!"

The words burned with a command that defied all resistance, and again Marshall found himself speaking.

"A plane," he said, "such as you smashed down when you rode the radio beam. It will carry her to New York.

She will be on that plane. You will find her on that plane. Even now she should be on her way."

Again the pressure seemed to be released. Again he was free of the monster's will. But it was too late. The radio robot now knew all it needed to know!

And suddenly, too, Marshall found he was once again able to move, once again able to breathe free of the strange radio-active shackles this creature had forged about his being. The heterodyning shrill rose in tempo, and the red metal body of the floating thing seemed to crackle with electrical vibrations—just as though gathering together power for momentum.

Marshall stood, frozen, then gasped as the robot reached out, took the record that was the key to its existence, the force that could call him from where he roved the ether, and smashed it, *deliberately*. It was as if the thing had said: "Now try to call me back!"

A sudden, blasting, raw-edged whine—and the thing was gone, with incredible speed! And once again the monster had moved in the line of quickest direction—straight through the concrete and steel of the station walls!

And again, the blanket of darkness that had enveloped the station was lifted. It was as if a fuse had been blown somewhere, and was now repaired. Lights flooded the room again!

MARSHALL paid scant attention to the ragged gap in the side of the wall, the gap through which the radio robot had hurtled, for the one thought in his mind was that of Sally. The robot was headed for Sally, seeking her, and knowing that she was on a plane bound for New York!

In three swift strides he was across the room and out into the hallway. Deserted, but an office door was ajar at the end of the hall. Marshall had some wild idea of calling the airport, chartering a plane immediately to overtake Sally's, as he headed for the open office door. And then, the sight of an electric clock above the door stopped him dead in his tracks.

The thing had been stopped, of course, during the time that the radio robot had been in the building. But the time to which the hands pointed gave Marshall a start. When he'd entered the building, there had been still an hour and a half before Sally's plane was to leave. An hour and a half.

Instantly, Marshall realized this, and realized, too that he had lost all track or sense of time during his encounter with the metal monster. But it couldn't have been an hour and a half. It couldn't have been that long.

Marshall cursed himself and looked at his wrist watch. In his haste and fear he had forgotten it completely. It wouldn't have been affected by the robot's presence—even though the electric clocks in the building had. By comparing the time of the stopped clock on the wall to his own watch, Marshall was able to approximate the length of its stay in the building. It had only been an hour. There was still half an hour left, a half an hour in which he might be able to stop Sally from boarding the plane. The plane which, somehow in his confusion, he had figured Sally already aboard.

There was a chance, although a scant one, that he might be able to reach Sally at the hotel. Marshall had moved into the office with the open door, even as he mentally considered this. An instant later and he was at the phone.

The desk clerk hesitated, while Marshall's heart hammered wildly in his chest, asking someone if Miss O'Neill had checked out yet. Then he came back on the wire.

"I think she's still in her room. I'll connect you," the clerk said over the phone. Marshall closed his eyes, praying silently that Sally was still there, while the receiver in his ear buzzed softly as the desk clerk tried to get her room on the switchboard.

SWEAT stood out in little beads on Marshall's forehead, and he ran a trembling hand nervously through his blonde hair as he waited. The very seconds seemed like separate eternities. Then—at last—he heard the click of the receiver in Sally's room being lifted.

"Sally!" Marshall was unable to keep the relief and overjoyed emotion from his voice.

The girl had instantly recognized Marshall's voice. For immediately she murmured something glacierally, and her voice was fading away as though she intended to hang up.

"*Sally!*" Marshall's tones were those of desperate urgency, and they must have communicated themselves to the girl, for she said stonily:

"Yes, what do you want? Please make it brief. I'm in a rush."

"Just that!" Marshall blurted, realizing that his haste would give him scant chance to put across what he had to say. "It's about your leaving, Sally. You can't do it. You mustn't. Please, I beg you!"

"Is that all you called for—a dramatic, amateurish, last-minute sob act?" Sally's voice was frigidity itself.

"But listen, Sally," Marshall was cursing himself desperately for the botch he was making of this. How could he tell her that some damned, grotesque monster was threatening her life—and make her believe it? The only thing he'd be able to do would be to stall her off. Try to make her stay in the hotel until he got there. Then it would be too late to take the plane. The plane for which the radio-robot was now more than likely searching the radio beams!

"Sally," he continued desperately. "Your life is in danger if you take that plane. I haven't time to tell you now. You must wait at the hotel until I get there! For the love of heaven, Sally, please listen to me!"

"As cheap gags go," he heard Sally's voice replying acidly, "that was rather good. Considering it came from someone so cheap himself!"

"Sally," Marshall was straining every effort of will to get his message to her, to make her believe him. But even as he spoke he knew it was useless to try to crack the shell she'd built to cover the hurt he'd inflicted on her. "Sally," he pleaded. "Listen to me, for the sake of what we used to feel, for the sake of what we once meant to one another—listen to me!"

"How touching. Really, you should try radio theatricals sometime," Sally's voice replied. "There's a lot of money in it for anyone who can make animal sounds—of the snake variety!"

"Sally," Marshall's voice was one last pleading effort, "You have to wait. Please! I can explain!"

"Sorry," Sally answered, and it seemed that the coating of ice to her tones had thickened with each reply. "Sorry, I'm in a hurry. I have a plane to catch. To New York. If what you have to say is really important, you might send it air mail—to your congressman!" The click of the receiver was quite final in its sound.

Marshall slammed the telephone down, gritting his teeth. She was starting for the airport. It was almost half an hour from the radio station to the airport, and less than that from the hotel to there.

There was one last chance—try to get to the airport before the plane left. He knew, as he rushed from the office, that Sally would arrive at the airport before him. He hoped that she wouldn't be gone—also—before him!

Dashing out of the station building, Marshall found a taxicab waiting on the corner. He clambered inside, stuffing a ten dollar bill into the startled driver's paw.

"The airport," he gasped, still breathing hard, "as fast as you can make it!"

The cabbie did his best—within the law. But there were stoplights, and no amount of persuasion on the part of Dan Marshall could induce him to break the law. They pulled into the airport just as a huge, tri-motored transport plane took off, rising eastward. Marshall was out of the cab, looking after the rising ship until it was lost in the darkness of the sky. Lost in the sky in which the robot waited for Sally!

CHAPTER FIVE
Killer in the Sky

FOR several stunned minutes, Dan Marshall stood there, gazing up at the vast black sky—fighting off the horrible realization that his chance of saving Sally had disappeared even as the tiny gray silhouette of the huge airliner had vanished in the gloom.

Gone—and there was no way to stop her. Even now the robot might—Marshall couldn't finish the thought. It was too ghastly. Not Sally. Sally couldn't die. He had to stop that plane—somehow!

And then Marshall wheeled, seized by a sudden daring idea—inspiration born of his frantic urgency. There was a way, a possibility, and anything was worth a gamble...

A message. A message along the radio beam would do it, might reach the plane in time to avert the certain disaster that lay ahead.

Marshall's long legs carried him swiftly across the landing field, past the depot waiting rooms, and up to the Airport Radio Room. Through the lighted window, Marshall could see two operators sitting over wireless keys inside the place. There was also a man in the uniform of an Army Lieutenant standing before a desk. Marshall barged through the door.

The Lieutenant, a tall, dark young fellow, turned quizzically at his hasty entrance. One of the operators looked up from the wireless key before him.

"I must get in touch with the airliner that just left for New York!" Dan said swiftly, loudly. "It's extremely urgent!"

The Lieutenant smiled curiously. "What's the trouble?"

Marshall started to speak, then cut off the words he had almost uttered. It would do no good to tell them the truth. They'd send no messages for madmen. And they would certainly think him mad if he babbled about robots and plane crashes. Desperately, he searched his brain for a logical excuse, something that would enable him to talk them into putting the message through.

"There's a girl aboard," Dan said, forming his idea as he spoke, "whose mother has taken ill, seriously! I must get in touch with her. I tell you, it's urgent. I must get a message to the ship." As he finished, Marshall was thinking swiftly. A message to the airliner might result in an emergency landing—he hoped. If he could get them to make such a landing, could put across his message, he might avert the robot's head-on crash with the airliner.

The Lieutenant nodded sympathetically. "We can send a message to the next airport—but that's all. As soon as she arrives there she'll receive it."

"But I've got to reach her in the plane, immediately!" Marshall's voice was frantic.

The Lieutenant shook his head. "Sorry. It's against communication orders. Airship wave lengths are to be used strictly for navigation communications between the ships and the ground stations. Besides, it wouldn't hasten matters any if the girl was to get the message in the plane. She'd have to wait until it landed at the next stop, anyway."

Marshall was already cursing himself inwardly for a blundering fool. His hastily constructed lie had been much too hasty, much too stupid, to aid his plans. He stood there, hesitating for an instant, then his hand, which had been groping about in his pocket, touched his automatic. The weapon was empty, and quite useless. But it might serve. In a swift motion, he drew, leveling the gun on the three startled occupants of the wireless room.

HE tried to keep both hand and voice steady as he held the gun on the three. "You'll send the message I tell you," Marshall snapped. He lifted the gun slightly, ominously.

The Lieutenant's tone was suddenly soft, deadly, as he said:

"Listen, fellow, I don't know what in hell this is all about, but you'd better put that thing down before it goes off. There'll be no messages sent from here. Don't be a fool!"

The wireless operators sat at their keys, faces turned in astonishment toward Dan, but there was no fear in their expressions. Marshall groaned inwardly. His threat was— like his gun—quite empty. His bluff had been called. These men, even though they must think him mad, were displaying cool courage.

And at that instant, even while he hesitated, the door behind Marshall was opened. Quickly, Marshall stepped to the side, gun still leveled on the three in the room, eyes flicking to the person who had just entered. The intruder was a man in greasy overalls, obviously an aviation mechanic. He didn't see Marshall, and spoke directly to the Lieutenant.

"Your ship is ready, Lieutenant," the mechanic said. "We've rolled her up on the ramp, and she's all set to go."

And then, noticing the fixed expression on the Lieutenant's face, the mechanic wheeled, saw Dan Marshall and the gun he held in his hand.

"Okay," Marshall snapped, waving the gun to include the mechanic, "step over beside the Lieutenant, and no tricks!"

A new idea—a daring scheme—had suddenly come to Marshall. It was born with the entering speech of the mechanic, and by the sight of the Lieutenant's overcoat and visored cap lying on a table less than five feet from where Dan stood. A ship, evidently an army plane, Dan was thinking. It would have a radio. It would—

He didn't need to reason any further. His own past in the air-mail service would come in handy now. He stepped to the table, still holding the gun on the others, and picked up the overcoat and visored cap. Clumsily, he kept the gun steady, and somehow managed to don the coat and cap.

This had consumed less than sixty seconds—one breathless minute while the four watched him in silent amazement. Now Marshall was at the door, still keeping them covered with the automatic.

"Okay, gentlemen," Marshall snapped. "I'm leaving, but I'll be looking over my shoulder for three or four minutes as I go. It won't be smart for anyone of you to stick your nose out the door of this shack until after that time!" Marshall had backed to the door, still open as the mechanic had left it. Now he stepped out onto the stoop. Then, quickly, he slammed the door shut on the men inside, wheeled, and dashed down the steps.

There was only one plane on the take-off ramp, and the ramp was less than a hundred yards from the shack. Marshall, burdened by the heavy army overcoat, made the ramp in a little over ten seconds. The mechanics who were around the U. S. Army fighting plane, were startled as Marshall drew up beside it.

"Okay," Dan snapped. "In a hurry. Let's get under way!"

To all appearances, Dan was an Army Officer, and the grease monkeys, though startled, helped him willingly into the cockpit. Then, as Marshall throttled the ship to greater life, he saw the blocks snapped away, and he gunned the plane down the runway.

Marshall took one quick look over his shoulder, before the tail lifted. One quick look that showed him four angry men dashing from the Airport Radio Room toward the now deserted take-off ramp!

And then Marshall was easing back on the stick, and the swift little combat ship climbed skyward as the black ground blotted off in darkness beneath him. Above, the starless sky waited tauntingly—as though challenging him to overtake the airliner, to get his message to the great ship before tragedy, stark calamity, struck at Sally O'Neill.

IN the pilot's compartment of the Transcontinental Airliner *Hawk*, the co-pilot at the radio board looked quizzically at his partner.

"I can't understand it, Clem," he said. "This damned static is increasing with every mile we make. "I'm having a helluva time trying to get the ground stations ahead. They just don't seem to come through, even though we're on the beam."

The pilot, a wide-shouldered, freckled, young blond, shook his head worriedly. "Try again," was all he said.

THE ATTRACTIVE young stewardess moved down the aisle of the *Hawk's* cabin smiling at the passengers, arranging pillows and pausing occasionally to answer questions.

She was passing along the aisle when a short, fat man caught her by the arm. The passenger list gave his name as "Ryker." He sat on the outside of the aisle, next to a lovely red-headed girl whom the list identified as "Miss Sally O'Neill."

"Listen, Stewardess," Ryker said, "aren't we traveling rather rough on this hop? Seems as if something might be haywire with our course."

The stewardess smiled reassuringly. "Not at all," she answered. "The weather's rough tonight, yes. But there isn't anything to worry about. We'll be into better conditions shortly."

Ryker nodded doubtfully. "I see," he said. "I guess so. I was just curious. Don't want anything to happen. This little lady here," he pointed to the redheaded girl beside him, "has to get to New York without delay. Got an important broadcast to make, and she can't afford to miss the only rehearsal she'll have."

The stewardess smiled again. "Miss O'Neill will arrive on schedule, never fear." Then she moved down the aisle as Ryker turned and began to speak to the girl.

THE FRECKLE-FACED pilot of the *Hawk* moved his wide shoulders restlessly and turned to the co-pilot. His voice was slightly uneasy as he spoke.

"Try to get that beam-call in a little clearer," he said. "It seems to me that we're not riding smoothly. There's no reason for static, unless there's an electrical storm ahead of us. Get in touch with the ground shack a hundred miles ahead. See if they've noticed anything."

The co-pilot moved his hands expressively. "Hell, Clem, I'm trying to do that. I've been trying for almost fifteen minutes. But this static condition is getting worse and worse."

The pilot shook his head bewilderedly. "For a radio beam, the points we're riding are about as smooth as a roller coaster. Keep trying."

Muttering inaudibly, the co-pilot went back to his radio.

DAN MARSHALL was giving the little combat ship a dose of hell. For fifteen minutes now, he'd torn the guts out of the motor in an effort to narrow down the distance between himself and the *Hawk*.

His mind was torn in an agony of anxiety and terrifying apprehension. Every single mile he'd put behind him had been this way. And he still had no sight of the *Hawk* ahead. Marshall had used the radio again and again, sending out frantic messages in the hope that the pilots of the huge transport plane might somehow receive them.

But there were indications which might mean a foreboding of disaster. For, from his radio, Dan Marshall was able to realize that the static conditions in the sky around him were growing steadily worse and worse. This meant but one thing—that he was getting closer and closer to Yolan. Obviously, the radio robot's prowling of the beam was responsible for these static conditions. Soon, perhaps, he might be close enough to get a message to the airliner. He'd *need* to be close to pierce the static!

But sooner than that, perhaps, the monster might find the *Hawk*—and Marshall dreaded to think of the results that would follow. He knew, now, that the situation had narrowed down to one premise. He would get to the transport ship before the robot did—or Yolan would find the plane before Marshall's message could reach it.

So there in the blackness of the night, two thousand feet above a mountain range, Marshall throttled his ship ahead, hoping, ever hoping, peering ahead in the darkness, until suddenly his eyes narrowed and his hope crystallized to an emotion approaching almost hysterical relief. Ahead of him, perhaps a mile and a half in the gray-black night, he saw the flickering sheen of silvered wings.

Frantically, almost sobbing, Marshall reached for his radio hook-up on the control board. Reached for it, then stopped midway, his hand clenching in sudden, awful horror. For far off in the distance, so far as to be but a tiny dancing spark, something was moving to meet the *Hawk*. And that something, beyond all shadow of doubt, was the Floating Robot!

It was growing—that dancing, meteor-like spark. Growing as Marshall watched in frozen terror. Growing as it hurtled at incredible speed along the beam; hurtled toward the big plane!

SOMEHOW, Marshall had the radio apparatus in his hand, was shouting into the ship's transmitter mike.

"Calling Airliner *Hawk*....Calling pilot on *Hawk*...Veer Off!...Veer, for God's sake!"

But the spark was growing until it was a monstrous ball of crackling electrical flame, hurtling blindly toward the airliner. Marshall was shouting into the transmitter mike, again and again, almost insanely. The silver winged transport ship suddenly was bobbing cork-like, this way and that, as the pilot apparently saw the swift menace approaching. He was descending now, trying to land.

Marshall's lungs were torn and hoarse, but he shouted again and again, as though he could, by the very volume of his voice, avert the terror of the impending catastrophe.

And then the hurtling ball of electrical hell was upon the great airliner—and suddenly, at the last instant, the *Hawk* was veering!

But it veered too late, for Marshall, even as his breath tore in his lungs, saw both ship and robot bob in the same direction! Even as the air became thick with crackling static, above it came the sickening sound of the great metal wing of the transport plane shearing!

Yolan had hit the wing—and the great ship was twisting earthward, swiftly falling, falling. Marshall groaned with the torment of a man in hell, and threw his hand across his face. He couldn't bear to watch it...couldn't...couldn't. His mind was lanced with agony. Sally...Sally...going down to her death!

Beneath, the cruel peaks of the mountain ranges waited; ready to embrace the falling plane, ready to gnash their fanged teeth into the twisted wreckage that would crumple there.

Marshall kicked his plane into a steep, twisting climb, blotting out the horror of the sight for a merciful instant. Numbing the agony that gripped his brain for an instant at least. And finally, leveling the ship out, Marshall forced himself to look over the side.

The wreck was down there on the snow-peaked crags— but incredibly, was not burning, was not torn asunder by the rock ridges! The wing was gone, but that had happened in midair, and now the ship lay on its belly, otherwise intact. By a miracle of skill the pilot had landed the ship! Dancing around it, though, was the crackling flaming ball that meant Yolan! And then Yolan shot away, into the forest!

And in that startled instant, Marshall dared to believe that the astonishing miracle had really happened—that

Sally, pray God, was still alive. For from the position of the ship, from the very appearance of it—there was a good chance that she was—a chance!

One glance was enough to show Marshall that there wasn't the slightest chance of his being able to land his ship on those mountain ridges. The attempt would mean instant death. The transport plane had settled there through miracle, but miracles didn't happen twice. There was, therefore, but one thing for Marshall to do. Get back to the airport. Get back as swiftly as wings could carry him, and report the crash, rescue the survivors from the crags, if they—if *she* still lived.

But suddenly Marshall realized that he couldn't return to the airport. He couldn't risk it—for at this very moment the hue and cry over his theft of the Army plane was probably under way. By now every field within flying range of the place was probably on the lookout for him. And soon—if it were not already a fact—there would be other ships searching the skyways for his pirated plane.

But he had to get back to the *Hawk*, had to get there before Sally—if she was still alive—fell victim to the floating robot. With every thought, Marshall tried desperately to make himself believe Sally still lived.

Marshall ruddered the fighting ship hard, pointed the nose back in the direction from which he'd come. Two things were now clear to him. He couldn't return to any legitimate landing field, and, should he manage to get to the *Hawk*, there would be only one way to defeat the robot. One way born around an inspiration that had occurred subconsciously to him less than a minute ago.

It was a wild scheme, perhaps an impossible one, but there was a chance of its working. And too, it would fit in perfectly with the fact that there was no legitimate field where he could land. For Marshall had remembered a field, a deserted, barren, bumpy long-undeveloped realty tract near the radio station. He would be able to land there—maybe. And from there it was less than ten minutes to the studios, where, he could organize the rest of his plan before he set out for the *Hawk*.

Less than a quarter of an hour later, Marshall—with the aid of God and good air sense—set the ship down on the deserted realty stretch. And in less than half that time, he was racing up the steps and into the radio station.

CHAPTER SIX
Death in the Mountains

THE ground was rushing at her. Saber-sharp crags reached up at her like the open jaws of some hungry beast.

Sally O'Neill jerked the crash belt tighter about her slim waist and breathed a silent prayer. It was only a matter of seconds before the *Hawk* would dash itself into splintered wreckage on those razor keen rocks.

"Ready," It was the Stewardess moving down the aisle. "Two hundred feet. Prepare for crash!"

"Damn it," Ryker screamed. "Do something, do y'hear, do something! I don't want to die."

There was no answer from her but Sally looked scornfully at the small, trembling figure of the radio executive.

"Why don't you jump?" she snapped. The next instant the plane brushed a high rock and a rending, splintering noise crashed into her eardrums.

"This is it!" someone shouted.

The ship nosed over sharply and then with sickening abruptness, its forward motion was checked. It was as if a giant hand had stretched out to catch the crashing ship.

Sally cried out as her entire weight strained against the narrow strap that circled her waist—then a mantle of blackness settled over her.

When she opened her eyes the plane was still, evidently resting in the ravine. Sally crawled to her feet, trying to pull her confused, bewildered wits together.

Her eardrums rang with shock and dizziness and she moved awkwardly to the door. One of the pilots was climbing from his seat shaking his head.

"It's crazy, impossible," he muttered.

Sally's hand was on the knob of the door when a heavy hand fell on her shoulder, spun her around and away from the door.

It was Ryker, his face twisted with hysterical fear.

"Out of my way," he screamed. "Let me out of here!"

HE jerked open the door and sprang to the ground, sobbing wildly. Sally started to follow him and then she stopped—her mouth opening in horror.

Something was floating toward the ship! A red and gold ball of metal, surrounded by white, crackling sparks and flame. Ominously, silently, it floated toward the ship as if directed by some evil, malignant intelligence.

Sally heard her own terror stricken scream ringing in her ears before she was aware that she had opened her mouth.

Ryker heard her and wheeled, his face going a pasty white as his eyes focused on the horrible apparition floating toward him.

"Keep away," he screamed. "For God's sake keep away." His voice broke into an hysterical, mouthing babble as he backed away from the silently advancing creature. Then he turned and fled, his hoarse bleating screams trailing over his shoulder.

For an instant the fiery monster seemed to hesitate, then it flashed after him, the huge metallic ball of energy whistling through the air like a meteor.

Sally screamed again. And then the creature of flame was on top of Ryker. A terrible bleating scream ripped through the air and Ryker was on the ground threshing horribly under the attack of the weird monster.

Sally covered her face with her hands. It was too awful. Her thoughts broke off suddenly and her heart seemed to swell in her chest until it would choke her. And even at that instant, she knew…

This creature, this weird, incredible apparition must be the thing that Dan had tried to warn her about. And it was looking for her! She stifled the scream of panic that welled in her throat and looked desperately about for some place to hide.

About a hundred yards from the plane a slope led to a ridge and beyond that the dark opening of a mining shaft was visible.

In an instant she was on the rough uneven ground, running, stumbling toward the shaft, toward safety. A frantic glance over her shoulder showed her the incredible figure of the radio robot still hovering over the now still body of Ryker.

Within fifty yards her breath was searing her lungs and throat like a hot blast from a furnace. Her heart hammered painfully against her ribs, but she couldn't stop. If she did— A sob wrenched itself from her throat as she pictured her fate at the mercies of the hideous fury of the radio robot!

HER high heels twisted and turned on the rocky, treacherous ground but somehow she managed to keep her feet, and stumble onward. The wind whipped her auburn-red hair over her face, blinding her, but she struggled on, desperately, frantically, knowing that her only slim chance was to keep running; to reach the comparative security of the mining shaft before the robot caught her.

Twenty feet from the entrance of the shaft she heard a hissing, roaring noise behind her. Twisting, she saw over her shoulder a huge, flaming ball of red and black fire, flashing about the ship, seemingly confused and baffled.

Sally sobbed a prayer of thankfulness and hurried up the few remaining feet that led to the sanctuary of the shaft. At the dark entrance she paused and looked back at the plane. The flaming robot was still circling the plane but suddenly its course veered. It was flashing away from the plane, hurtling over the ground toward the entrance of the shaft!

Sally fought back a scream. Somehow the creature had discovered her trail, and was flashing with incredible speed toward her. For the briefest flicker of a second, she remained paralyzed with fright, then she wheeled and ran into the shaft.

Stygian blackness enveloped her immediately. She fled through the shaft, her feet finding footing by a miracle. She knew she was running downhill, toward the center of the mountain; and she was also aware that she was running on rail tracks, for her heels caught and twisted on the ties. And suddenly her heel caught and held, her ankle twisted sharply, throwing her to the ground. For a second she couldn't move, and then she crawled to her feet, looked fearfully back up the shaft. There was a queer flickering illumination at the mouth of the tunnel and then the radio robot was in sight, its hissing, crackling, red and gold body silhouetted in terrible clarity against the blackness of the night.

Sally whimpered in terror, but she did not quit. Wheeling, she ran again, her breath escaping her throat in great sobs. Behind her she could hear a terrible noise that sounded like the crackling of a mighty blaze. Then by the flickering eerie light that was illuminating the tunnel she saw a tunnel siding branching off to her left. Without thinking, she hurled herself to the ground, crawled into the siding. Quivering with terror she crouched helplessly against the rough wall of rock and waited…

THE noise at the mouth of the shaft was growing in volume and then the tunnel itself was filled with the roaring ominous noise. The entire shaft trembled slightly and then with the speed of a meteor and the noise of an express train, the floating robot flashed past her, and disappeared into the bowels of the earth.

It was hunting, Sally knew, for her! Trembling, she crawled to her feet and bumped into a hard, heavy object. She saw that it was a small car loaded with ore, set on the siding track. Moving around it, the idea came to her. It was wild but—

She ran to the front of the ore car and jerked out the wooden blocks from under the wheels. Then she hurried to the rear of the car, her pulses throbbing madly. Bending low she braced her shoulder against the grab-iron of the car and shoved with all of her weight and strength. For a terrible second the car remained motionless, then it was rolling slowly, the rails creaking protestingly under its weight.

Sally panted exultantly as the car gathered momentum and speed. With a final shove she sent it rolling onto the tracks of the main shaft. It gathered speed swiftly and with a rattling, metallic roar, sped down the rails—*after the floating robot!*

Sally watched as it rocked and rattled down the rails. And then it happened.

The car was off the trail, plowing along the track and ripping into the soft shale shoulder that flanked the tunnel. Sparks flew, a steady roar filled the tunnel, then tons of dirt and ore were collapsing from the walls and ceilings, burying the car under their weight.

Sally watched, held in horrified fascination as boulders and rocks piled together in a jarring, shattering tangle, completely sealing the tunnel. Sally sobbed in relief. The thing, the weird apparition that had menaced her, was down there buried under tons of rock and dirt. Blocked off!

The noise of the crash slowly trembled away into silence, but she was aware then of another noise. A steady, burring noise that filled the darkness with an angry crackling sound. It seemed to come from deep under the debris and to be heading with irresistible power toward her.

Sally trembled. It was the creature, she knew, burrowing relentlessly forward. It hadn't been destroyed by the cave-in, merely enraged, momentarily blocked off.

She wheeled then and ran for the mouth of the shaft. In the darkness she didn't see the beam. It was slipping from its place and she darted under it.

A hard, unyielding weight crashed into her shoulder, and Sally O'Neill felt nothing more but blackness.

THE tiny truck thundered around a sharp, banked turn on the white ribbon of highway, but Dan Marshall, at the wheel, didn't lessen his pressure on the accelerator the slightest. From the instant he'd entered the station, he had worked swiftly, desperately. And now he was driving wildly, torn by an anxiety of impatience, as the burning tires of the truck ate up mile after mile, racing against time.

The speedometer needle wavered at eighty, while the tiny truck two-wheeled, then righted itself. Now Dan straightened out around the turn, and the speedometer needle crawled slowly, surely, to ninety-five—the maximum speed that the little vehicle could reach.

Hearing the equipment in the back of the truck slide perilously to one side, Marshall breathed a swift prayer that none of it should be damaged. And then he cursed inwardly, for he still was uncertain that he'd ever have the opportunity to use it. If Sally had been harmed, if Sally wasn't alive when he reached the wreck! Marshall shuddered at the thought, his foot mashing the accelerator until it seemed as though he were pushing it through the floorboards.

The roads were growing steeper and with every twisting turn the tiny truck creaked protestingly against the ruthless treatment it was receiving. Marshall, if he noticed this, was not concerned. His face, twisted in anxiety, was fixed rigidly on the road ahead of him. Somewhere along here there should be a highway siding—a siding leading to a bumpy gravel off-road. That gravel route would take him to the scene of the airliner's crash.

And then, rushing up at him, and caught for an instant in the white glare of his headlights, Marshall saw the signboard that told him the gravel road was less than a quarter of a mile away. Ten seconds later, Marshall had slowed the truck enough to throw it into a sliding, crunching, sickening turn that brought him around facing the road siding. Then, throwing the truck into second, he was thundering ahead toward the gravel off-road.

Minutes later, Marshall's truck was bumping perilously, recklessly, along the gravel road. It was as steep and winding as it was bumpy, bleak trees hemming it in along the sides. Marshall knew, now, that he had to run the risk of damaging the equipment, had to sacrifice everything, risk all, in his efforts to beat Time.

Four miles ahead, four miles in which the truck had climbed better than a thousand feet, Marshall heard a sound that made him instantly kill the motor and leap from the truck—a hoarse shout, coming from deep back in the roadside, behind the thick maze of forest!

And as he stood there, beside the truck, looking uncertainly right and left through the darkness, the shout was repeated.

"Hallllooooooo, there! Hellllllllllp, halllooooo!"

Marshall had placed the sound, and was barging off the road and into the underbrush of forest, heading for the voice, shouting himself, "Coming! Coming!"

Three hundred feet later, Marshall emerged from the forest underbrush and stood at the edge of a clearing that marked a narrow mountain ravine. He gasped a sobbing cry of relief—for there in the clearing was the wreck of the *Hawk*, and surrounding it were the survivors of the disaster...

MARSHALL was running across the clearing, and one of the group huddled beside the plane was coming to meet him. From the fellow's dress, Marshall knew him for one of the pilots.

And then, while Marshall stood beside him, the fellow was babbling incoherently, clutching frantically to his arm, his face white and torn with strain.

"Thank heavens you've come! Where are the rest? We're going crazy…all of us. Terrible! One of the passengers, a man, was gruesomely torn apart by some hideous thing… A girl…ran like hell toward the forest edge, up a grade leading to that old mine there," the pilot pointed. "Don't know how we were cushioned into our landing…shouldda been killed…all of us…a monster…a crackling thing from hell I tell you…followed the girl after killing that guy…we all saw it…can't be crazy! Damn, it's been a nightmare. Been next to the plane ever since. Didn't dare separate…"

Then the rest of them had gotten courage enough to come beside Marshall, were surrounding him, all of them babbling in wild hysteria, their faces white with ghastly fear. And Marshall, piecing the story together as swiftly as he could, got the entire picture. Primarily, the robot was still in the vicinity, Sally was still alive—*and both had disappeared toward that mine on the side of the mountain ridge!*

Dan Marshall didn't hesitate; he took instant command of the situation. His words lashed the frightened group into a dull, completely bewildered subservience.

Three male passengers and the pilot carried the co-pilot, who had a broken leg, back to the truck, while the stewardess shepherded the others—a little girl and four women—along also. They left them in the truck, while the three men, with Marshall's aid and direction, unloaded the mobile equipment from the back of the tiny vehicle. They were dazed, all of them, and uncomprehending.

"We'll have to carry it back to the clearing, up the side of that mountain ridge to the deserted mine shaft!" Marshall snapped.

"But, wha—" the pilot began.

"The girl, you fool," Marshall's voice was harsh with the anxiety that tore at him, "She's up there, and that 'thing' you saw is up there too. We're going after it. And I'm going to need this equipment badly…"

The pilot seemed about to protest no further, but one of the three male passengers, a bald, fat little man, squealed indignation. And suddenly the pilot had him by the lapels, shaking him violently. "You heard him," he grated. "We're all pitching in. Let's get going!"

Dan Marshall had time for one brief, humorless grin of thanks, then, as swiftly as they could move under their burdens, the little group started through the forest underbrush and back to the clearing and the wreckage. Marshall led the way, now, with the pilot directly behind him.

They were across the clearing, past the crumpled hulk of the airliner, and starting up the mountain ridge that led to the deserted mine. Somewhere up there, Dan Marshall knew, the metal robot monster sought Sally O'Neill.

AND then they stood on the ridge, all of them breathing heavily from their exertions, looking right and left in apprehension. But Marshall hadn't hesitated. The gaping opening that marked the entrance to the mine seemed to beckon, and even as he approached it he heard a faint, distant crackling coming from its darkened recesses. The radio robot was in there, and so, therefore, was Sally!

Marshall turned to shout to the others, but his mouth had half-opened when there came another, louder and more ominous sound from the shaft. A distant rumbling, increasing in volume as it swept along to the throat of the tunnel—a cave in!

Face white with sudden, terrible apprehension, Marshall shouted to the pilot.

"For God's sake, get over here with the stuff! They're in there!"

The rumble had grown fainter, but Marshall thought he could still hear rock falling inside the tunnel. He caught the choking breath of ore dust that rushed out at him. While the others brought the equipment to the mouth of the mine tunnel, Marshall worked swiftly, desperately, reeling out foot after foot of portable microphone wire—fighting off the terrible premonitions that seared his mind.

Then, flashlight in hand, microphone strapped to his chest, Dan Marshall turned to the others. "Whatever happens, wait here," he ordered. "If I don't come out—you'll know what to do!"

And with that, Marshall stepped into the inky tunnel, snapping his flashlight, throwing its rays down the long slope. For his first ten strides, the searching white finger revealed nothing. Revealed nothing as a sudden pounding reverberated from back in the tunnel. Then, as Marshall cried aloud in a hysteria of relief, the flashlight's ray caught Sally!

The girl was on the floor of the shaft, lying perhaps a hundred feet ahead, pinned back against the water-soaked walls by a thick, heavy prop beam!

For an awful moment this scene stamped itself on Marshall's brain like some nightmarish panorama. Then he saw more. The girl was unconscious, and lay limply twisted beneath the weight of the huge wooden beam. But behind her, less than two hundred feet, was the place where the cave in had occurred—the place from which even now the thunderous pounding was coming!

And through the debris of stone and buckled timber proppings, on the other side of that cave-in—was the floating radio robot! Marshall saw faint sparks and heard angry crackling as the creature hurled itself again and again in prodigious efforts to break through the slag slide to where they were!

Now Marshall was beside the girl, while the monster continued to rain great blows on the debris that blocked him off. Marshall had Sally's head cradled in his arms, and was sobbing half-hysterically in relief as he realized she was still alive. The shock, the fright, perhaps a blow from the falling beam, had stunned her into unconsciousness. But she was still alive!

The hammering of the monster grew louder, and looking up wildly, Marshall saw that the timbers blocking the creature's path were slowly giving way before the terrific assault. The radio monstrosity was breaking through…

The crackling static-like flashes were increasing in a sort of frenzied fury as the thing gained progress, inch-by-inch, through the block-off.

Frantically, Marshall bent over the girl. But in an instant he saw that it would take the efforts of three men to move the beam from her. And then, suddenly, he remembered the microphone strapped to his chest. His scheme— But, even as he thought of it, even as the momentarily forgotten plan returned to him, he knew it was now useless!

Useless, because it had depended on the voice of Sally O'Neill—and now Sally lay inertly in his arms, unable to utter a word, let alone the note that was their one weapon against the monster!

MARSHALL bit savagely into his lower lip, cursing the gods of fate that had done this to him, the terrible mocking fate that grinned evilly down on them in challenge to avert the menace that would destroy them both before another minute had passed.

"Sally, Sally," he sobbed desperately. "Oh God, girl, I can't get you out of this I—" his voice broke off, and he drew her head to his chest.

At that instant, even as Marshall's horrified gaze saw the crackling monster shatter the last of the debris that had been holding it off, Sally O'Neill stirred. Stirred, and moved her head back to look dazedly up into the face of Dan Marshall—and in the next instant to look toward the hammering, crackling monster.

As the thing smashed through the last of the barrier, and hung suspended like some glowing, horrible picture of Death—Sally O'Neill screamed shrilly!

The next scene would be stamped on Dan Marshall's memory through eternity. There was a vast, roaring, ear-splitting, tremendous detonation. Splashes of static flame shot everywhere along the shaft, blinding in the lightning-like vividness of them. The floating monster, engulfed in the vortex of this holocaust disintegrated into a myriad shower of blazing sparks.

And then all was black…

SALLY WAS SOBBING against Dan Marshall's chest. "Don't worry, darling," he said gently, "it's all over now. It's gone, forever destroyed. There'll be no more radio robot—ever."

Sally shuddered. "But my scream, you said my scream was responsible—" she began.

Marshall broke in: "That scream hit precisely the same pitch as the high note in the aria. And it was through that high note that I'd intended to hurl the monster back into the ether. The telephone voice-scrambling device I brought in the truck from the station took care of the rest. It hurled the pieces of the creature into a thousand different aerial waves."

But Sally O'Neill, ever the woman, was losing interest in the explanation. Obviously, she was far more concerned with the man who held her in his arms—the man who stopped talking now to kiss her again.

THE END

If you've enjoyed this book, you will not want to miss these terrific titles…

ARMCHAIR SCI-FI & HORROR DOUBLE NOVELS, $12.95 each

D-11   **PERIL OF THE STARMEN** by Kris Neville
THE STRANGE INVASION by Murray Leinster

D-12   **THE STAR LORD** by Boyd Ellanby
CAPTIVES OF THE FLAME by Samuel R. Delany

D-13   **MEN OF THE MORNING STAR** by Edmond Hamilton
PLANET FOR PLUNDER by Hal Clement and Sam Merwin, Jr.

D-14   **ICE CITY OF THE GORGON** by Chester S. Geier and Richard Shaver
WHEN THE WORLD TOTTERED by Lester del Rey

D-15   **WORLDS WITHOUT END** by Clifford D. Simak
THE LAVENDER VINE OF DEATH by Don Wilcox

D-16   **SHADOW ON THE MOON** by Joe Gibson
ARMAGEDDON EARTH by Geoff St. Reynard

D-17   **THE GIRL WHO LOVED DEATH** by Paul W. Fairman
SLAVE PLANET by Laurence M. Janifer

D-18   **SECOND CHANCE** by J. F. Bone
MISSION TO A DISTANT STAR by Frank Belknap Long

D-19   **THE SYNDIC** by C. M. Kornbluth
FLIGHT TO FOREVER by Poul Anderson

D-20   **SOMEWHERE I'LL FIND YOU** by Milton Lesser
THE TIME ARMADA by Fox B. Holden

ARMCHAIR SCIENCE FICTION CLASSICS, $12.95 each

C-4   **CORPUS EARTHLING**
by Louis Charbonneau

C-5   **THE TIME DISSOLVER**
by Jerry Sohl

C-6   **WEST OF THE SUN**
by Edgar Pangborn

ARMCHAIR SCI-FI & HORROR GEMS SERIES, $12.95 each

G-1   **SCIENCE FICTION GEMS, Vol. One**
Isaac Asimov and others

G-2   **HORROR GEMS, Vol. One**
Carl Jacobi and others

If you've enjoyed this book, you will not want to miss these terrific titles...

ARMCHAIR SCI-FI & HORROR DOUBLE NOVELS, $12.95 each

D-21   **EMPIRE OF EVIL** by Robert Arnette
          THE SIGN OF THE TIGER by Alan E. Nourse & J. A. Meyer

D-22   **OPERATION SQUARE PEG** by Frank Belknap Long
          ENCHANTRESS OF VENUS by Leigh Brackett

D-23   **THE LIFE WATCH** by Lester del Rey
          CREATURES OF THE ABYSS by Murray Leinster

D-24   **LEGION OF LAZARUS** by Edmond Hamilton
          STAR HUNTER by Andre Norton

D-25   **EMPIRE OF WOMEN** by John Fletcher
          ONE OF OUR CITIES IS MISSING by Irving Cox

D-26   **THE WRONG SIDE OF PARADISE** by Raymond F. Jones
          THE INVOLUNTARY IMMORTALS by Rog Phillips

D-27   **EARTH QUARTER** by Damon Knight
          ENVOY TO NEW WORLDS by Keith Laumer

D-28   **SLAVES TO THE METAL HORDE** by Milton Lesser
          HUNTERS OUT OF TIME by Joseph E. Kelleam

D-29   **RX JUPITER SAVE US** by Ward Moore
          BEWARE THE USURPERS by Geoff St. Reynard

D-30   **SECRET OF THE SERPENT** by Don Wilcox
          CRUSADE ACROSS THE VOID by Dwight V. Swain

ARMCHAIR SCIENCE FICTION CLASSICS, $12.95 each

C-7   **THE SHAVER MYSTERY, Book One**
         by Richard S. Shaver

C-8   **THE SHAVER MYSTERY, Book Two**
         by Richard S. Shaver

C-9   **MURDER IN SPACE** by David V. Reed
         by David V. Reed

ARMCHAIR MASTERS OF SCIENCE FICTION SERIES, $16.95 each

M-3   **MASTERS OF SCIENCE FICTION, Vol. Three**
         Robert Sheckley, "The Perfect Woman" and other tales

M-4   **MASTERS OF SCIENCE FICTION, Vol. Four**
         Mack Reynolds, "Stowaway" and other tales

If you've enjoyed this book, you will not want to miss these terrific titles...

ARMCHAIR SCI-FI & HORROR DOUBLE NOVELS, $12.95 each

D-121   **THE GENIUS BEASTS** by Frederik Pohl
THIS WORLD IS TABOO by Murray Leinster

D-122   **THE COSMIC LOOTERS** by Edmond Hamilton
WANDL THE INVADER by Ray Cummings

D-123   **ROBOT MEN OF BUBBLE CITY** by Rog Phillips
DRAGON ARMY by William Morrison

D-124   **LAND BEYOND THE LENS** by S. J. Byrne
DIPLOMAT-AT-ARMS by Keith Laumer

D-125   **VOYAGE OF THE ASTEROID, THE** by Laurence Manning
REVOLT OF THE OUTWORLDS by Milton Lesser

D-126   **OUTLAW IN THE SKY** by Chester S. Geier
LEGACY FROM MARS by Raymond Z. Gallun

D-127   **THE GREAT FLYING SAUCER INVASION** by Geoff St. Reynard
THE BIG TIME by Fritz Leiber

D-128   **MIRAGE FOR PLANET X** by Stanley Mullen
POLICE YOUR PLANET by Lester del Rey

D-129   **THE BRAIN SINNER** by Alan E. Nourse
DEATH FROM THE SKIES by A. Hyatt Verrill

D-130   **CRY CHAOS** by Dwight V. Swain
THE DOOR THROUGH SPACE By Marion Zimmer Bradley

ARMCHAIR SCIENCE FICTION CLASSICS, $12.95 each

C-55   **UNDER THE TRIPLE SUNS**
by Stanton A. Coblentz

C-56   **STONE FROM THE GREEN STAR**
by Jack Williamson

C-57   **ALIEN MINDS**
by E. Everett Evans

ARMCHAIR SCI-FI & HORROR GEMS SERIES, $12.95 each

G-13   **SCIENCE FICTION GEMS, Vol. Seven**
Jack Vance and others

G-14   **HORROR GEMS, Vol. Seven**
Robert Bloch and others

If you've enjoyed this book, you will not want to miss these terrific titles...

ARMCHAIR SCI-FI & HORROR DOUBLE NOVELS, $12.95 each

D-131 **COSMIC KILL** by Robert Silverberg
BEYOND THE END OF SPACE by John W. Campbell

D-132 **THE DARK OTHER** by Stanley Weinbaum)
WITCH OF THE DEMON SEAS by Poul Anderson

D-133 **PLANET OF THE SMALL MEN** by Murray Leinster
MASTERS OF SPACE by E. E. "Doc" Smith & E. Everett Evans

D-134 **BEFORE THE ASTEROIDS** by Harl Vincent
SIXTH GLACIER, THE by Marius

D-135 **AFTER WORLD'S END** by Jack Williamson
THE FLOATING ROBOT by David Wright O'Brien

D-136 **NINE WORLDS WEST** by Paul W. Fairman
FRONTIERS BEYOND THE SUN by Rog Phillips

D-137 **THE COSMIC KINGS** by Edmond Hamilton
LONE STAR PLANET by H. Beam Piper & John J. McGuire

D-138 **BEYOND THE DARKNESS** by S. J. Byrne
THE FIRELESS AGE by David H. Keller, M. D.

D-139 **FLAME JEWEL OF THE ANCIENTS** by Edwin L. Graber
THE PIRATE PLANET by Charles W. Diffin

D-140 **ADDRESS: CENTAURI** by F. L. Wallace
IF THESE BE GODS by Algis Budrys

ARMCHAIR SCIENCE FICTION & HORROR CLASSICS, $12.95 each

C-58 **THE WITCHING NIGHT**
by Leslie Waller

C-59 **SEARCH THE SKY**
by Frederick Pohl and C. M. Kornbluth

C-60 **INTRIGUE ON THE UPPER LEVEL**
by Thomas Tempel Hoyne

ARMCHAIR SCI-FI & HORROR GEMS SERIES, $12.95 each

G-15 **SCIENCE FICTION GEMS, Vol. Eight**
Keith Laumer and others

G-16 **HORROR GEMS, Vol. Eight**
Algernon Blackwood and others